EDWIN SPENCER

EDWIN SPENCER
SHADOW MAGIC

J. D. IRWIN

Catnip

CATNIP BOOKS
Published by Catnip Publishing Ltd
14 Greville Street
London EC1N 8SB

This edition first published 2011
1 3 5 7 9 10 8 6 4 2

Cover illustration by Andy Parker
Cover design by Mandy Norman

A CIP catalogue record for this book is available from the
British Library.

ISBN 978-1-84647-133-9

Printed in Poland

www.catnippublishing.co.uk

For Lizzie

PROLOGUE

The young wizard tiptoed into the throne room, and the prince stood up.

'Bellwin, thank you for coming. You *are* alone?'

'Yes, Prince Auvlin. What is it? You look a little worried.'

'I need a great favour, my friend.'

'Why, of course. Does the king also need my help?'

'This is between only a few of us. It must be kept secret from my father.'

The wizard hesitated, then nodded. 'I see. What do you want me to do?'

'I am going to send someone to Earth. I need you to create the vortex.'

'But . . . but I would need Master Ollwin's permission.'

'That is not possible! Can you do it now? Can you do it here?'

The wizard looked around and wrung his hands.

'It is very important,' the prince persisted. 'Do this, and then I will tell you *why*.'

The door creaked. Someone was outside in the passage, waiting.

Bellwin glanced at Auvlin, then held up his left hand. 'Livre ignatia vortex,' he said, and a hazy circle of flame appeared behind the throne. Bellwin felt someone push past him, and a man walked towards the glow.

'Two days,' Auvlin said anxiously. 'No more than two days.'

The man disappeared into the vortex and there was a dull boom. The circle of flame shrank.

'Thank you,' Auvlin said. 'Now, Bellwin, I will tell you everything.'

CHAPTER ONE

Edwin Spencer didn't know much, but he was sure of one thing – he hadn't got an A for science last year by memorising the periodic table. He'd got it in return for impersonating a prince. Not an English prince – not the sort you'd see on a fancy mug or the ten o'clock news. A prince in another world.

Trouble was, only two other people in Templeton Grove knew this. And Edwin's mother wasn't one of them.

'ED-*WIN!*'

It was the first day of the new school year, and Mrs Spencer bustled into the kitchen with the post.

'*Young Scientist* . . . *Teen Chemist Gazette*. Where's *Adolescent Astronomer*?' She whacked Edwin across the back of the head. 'You haven't given it straight to Perpetua Allbright again?'

Jenny, the eldest Spencer child, scoffed. 'Why not? She's got more use for it that *him*. Tell us, Ed – how did you get that A for science? No wonder Mr Lorius disappeared. He must've been mad to give *you* a mark like *that*!'

Katie, her sister, agreed. 'Yeah . . . stark staring bonkers!'

Ollie, the youngest of the Spencer children, just cackled through a mouthful of toast.

'ENOUGH!'

Mrs Spencer thumped *Child Prodigy Monthly* onto the table. 'I will not have Edwin's achievements diminished!'

'I think you'll find, Mother,' Jenny remarked, 'that it's achievement. Singular.'

'No matter!' Mrs Spencer sniffed and laid a hand on Edwin's shoulder. 'Somewhere in this boy there *is* genius.'

Edwin sighed. That science mark had been more trouble than it was worth.

'Jenny's right – that A was a fluke,' he said for what felt like the hundredth time. 'I'm not going to get anywhere near it again.' And certainly not with Mr Harper in charge.

Mrs Spencer leaned down. 'No, Edwin,' she whispered, her bleached moustache bristling along her lip like a tie-dyed caterpillar. 'Mr Lorius *understood you*. Now –' She poked a wrapped-up journal in Edwin's face. '– read this on the bus.'

It wasn't until the journey home from school that Edwin took the magazine out of his bag. Well, his mother hadn't said *which* bus. But as the number 22 trundled down the High Street Edwin was deep in thought. It was this time last year that the strange Mr Lorius had started at Templeton Grove Comp. Even now it was hard to believe he was from another world, and that he'd come to take Edwin back there with him.

Hysteria, the place was called. It wasn't full of spaceships and force fields, as Edwin might've expected. The Hysterians lived in castles, rode horses and fought with spears and swords. And they used magic. Not card tricks, like Uncle Ernie did once at a Christmas party when someone spilled beer on the CD player – it was *real* magic.

Hysteria had a king called Janus. His only son and heir, Prince Auvlin, had been killed – or so the Hysterians thought – in mysterious circumstances, and without a successor to the throne Hysteria was vulnerable to attack from their enemy, the Umbrians.

Edwin looked *exactly* like Prince Auvlin, and Janus had asked Edwin to take his son's place to buy the Hysterians time. Edwin had gone to Hysteria, mistakenly taking science-whizz Perpetua Allbright with him, and together they'd saved the kingdom, bringing the real Prince Auvlin back to life in the process. Even now, Edwin couldn't quite believe it had happened.

Apart from Edwin and Perpetua, only his best friend, Nat, knew anything about it. Because the Hysterians were able to rewind time on Earth, no one even realised Edwin had been away. Of course everyone on the planet had to relive those weeks again, but all they experienced were vague flashes of memory. The TV and newspapers had called it *mass déjà vu*.

Edwin got off the bus just as the sun came out. He put down his bag to undo his coat, and out of the corner of his eye noticed someone sidle behind a tree. Edwin looked left then right, stepped off the pavement and caught a glimpse of a bearded man; Edwin looked directly at him and the man stared back.

Edwin crossed the road. The man crossed after him. Edwin quickened his pace. The man stepped up a gear. Edwin's heart began to race. He veered around a corner, his rucksack bouncing off his shoulder as he caught sight of his house. Edwin looked behind him. The man had gained ground. His eyes were wide . . . his face was flushed. Edwin began to run . . .

'Master Edwin – I am sent by Prince Auvlin!'

Edwin's stomach lurched. He spun around and the man slowed.

'You *what*?' Edwin whispered.

The man took a faltering step. 'I am sent by Prince Auvlin,' he repeated. 'My name is Rownan . . . I am High Woodsman to the Hysterian Court.'

Edwin glanced both ways along the road. Was this a joke? Had someone at school heard him and Perpetua talking? Edwin looked the man up and down – he certainly looked the part.

'So that's where you're from – Hysteria?' Edwin said cautiously.

'Yes, Master Edwin . . . *of course*.'

'How do I know you're telling the truth? How did you get here?'

'I came through the vortex.'

Edwin's eyes narrowed. 'What was it like?'

'It was full of fire at first. Then the fire disappeared, and it became very cold.'

Edwin took a deep breath. The man's description was Hysteria's vortex – to a tee. He swallowed. 'So . . . so what do they want?'

Before Rownan could answer, Edwin's front door swung open.

'EDWIN!' Mrs Spencer's voice shrieked. 'Who are you talking to?'

Rownan backed away.

'Er, it's . . . it's one of the science technicians,' Edwin

13

stumbled. 'He was just on his way to help Nat with his coursework.'

Mrs Spencer suddenly appeared, her smile wide, her enormous teeth glinting in the autumn sunshine.

'Oh, he-llo,' she gushed, rushing to the gate. 'Cornelia Spencer. *So* pleased to meet you. Do you have five minutes? I've spoken to Mr Harper *no end* of times, but he's always rather cagey about Edwin's performance. I'm sure you'd be *much* more forthcoming!'

'No!' Edwin blurted. 'He's got to go. Nat's *desperate* for help!'

Mrs Spencer gave a smug smile. 'Ah, well,' she cooed, 'some student's needs are greater than ours.' She patted Edwin's head. 'We can't *all* be scientific geniuses, can we, Mr . . . ?'

Edwin glanced at Rownan. 'Mr Beard,' he said quickly.

Mrs Spencer blinked. 'Oh, how unusual. Well, I'll let you get on, Mr Beard. But we must meet very soon – Mr Harper's comments require elaboration!'

Edwin tugged at Rownan's sleeve as his mother walked inside. 'Come on,' he muttered. 'Forget the Umbrians. *That* is probably one of the luckiest escapes you'll ever have.'

CHAPTER TWO

After dinner, Edwin told his mother he was going to Perpetua's house to study. She made him take a back copy of *Young Scientist*.

'You need to show the Allbrights you're serious,' she trilled. 'You're mixing in exalted circles now!'

As soon as Perpetua opened her front door, she guessed something was up.

'What is it?' she hissed as she dragged Edwin towards the study.

'Someone from Hysteria came for me,' he whispered as she bundled him inside.

'You're kidding!'

'Would I joke about it?'

Perpetua's eyes glinted. 'What do they want this time?'

'It's Prince Auvlin,' Edwin replied, flopping into a chair.

'He came *here*?' Perpetua gasped. 'That's a bit risky!'

'Not *him* – he sent some bloke called Rownan who said he worked for Janus, as a *woodsman* or something.'

Perpetua sat on the floor and crossed her legs. 'I don't remember him. So what did he say?'

Edwin rubbed his chin, trying to collect his thoughts.

'Well, Auvlin's going to represent Hysteria in a competition – some sort of triathlon – and although he's pretty much back to full strength, he's a bit worried about one of the disciplines.'

'Which one?'

'Orienteering – he wants to compete, but he's having trouble with his sense of direction.'

Perpetua rolled her eyes. 'What does he expect?' she said. 'He spent three months lying in a mausoleum. A state of near-death suspension isn't natural, you know – *something* was going to be affected.'

Edwin smirked. 'Could've been worse though, eh? He might've turned into a prize know-it-all.'

Perpetua glared. 'Just get to the point.'

'Right.' Edwin thought about what Rownan had told him. 'Auvlin doesn't want Janus to know there's something up with him, because he doesn't want him to worry. *And* it sounds really important that he wins this competition. That's where *I* come in.'

'And are you going to do it?' Perpetua clapped her hands. 'You might even win! Remember how quickly you found your way around Emporium Castle last time – your orienteering skills are fantastic!'

'Just about the *only* thing I'm any good at,' Edwin said meekly.

'Don't say that,' Perpetua replied, wagging her finger. 'You saved the Hysterians' bacon last year.'

Edwin grinned. 'Don't you mean their hog's buttock?' It was the closest thing the Hysterians had to bacon.

'Oh, yes! I'd forgotten about that! So,' Perpetua added, her tone becoming serious again, '*are* you going to compete for him?'

'I haven't decided yet . . . I mean we'd be deceiving Janus, and winning some triathlon doesn't seem a good reason to go back. Last time it was all about war with the Umbrians.'

Perpetua frowned. 'But you did say this trial *seemed important* . . . and maybe Auvlin's desperate not to worry his father. Surely he wouldn't waste precious magic sending Rownan through the vortex on a whim.'

Edwin shrugged, but Perpetua didn't give up. 'There's obviously not going to be any danger like there was the last time.' She tilted her head. 'Helping Janus made you feel good, didn't it?'

Edwin looked down. Not just good. It had been *wonderful*.

'And helping Auvlin might feel just the same!'

'I don't think so,' Edwin said quickly. 'We hardly knew him. Janus was . . . well, he was kind of like my *father*. Don't think it'd be worth going if I didn't see him.'

Perpetua nodded. 'I know how you feel about Janus,' she said softly. 'All the more reason I think you should jump at the chance to go back! Although if all this is secret, we *won't* be staying at the castle. Right?'

'No, Rownan said I could stay at his lodge with . . .' Edwin frowned. 'Oi! What's with the *we?*'

Perpetua shrugged, all innocent. 'I'd come with you, of course. If we're staying in the forest, there must be *so* many plants and animals to look at. I bet there's lots of different species that we don't have here. And there might be horse riding again. Come on! We've loved our lessons at the stables since we got back. And you've got really good!'

Edwin tut-tutted. Perpetua was trying to butter him up. 'I should've known I'd be lumbered with you if I ever went back to Hysteria.' He shrugged. 'OK. If I go, you can come too.'

'Oh, good! When would it be?'

'This triathlon starts in two weeks. I'd have loads of stuff to learn, so I've agreed to meet Rownan outside my house tomorrow after school. If I've decided to go, I'll do it then with him.'

Perpetua did a little dance. 'Fantastic! We can squeeze in Mr Harper's test beforehand.'

'Deep joy,' Edwin sighed. There were times he wondered if he and Perpetua had anything in common at all. 'We'll have to go through the vortex again, you know . . . .'

'Oh, that's fine,' Perpetua said breezily. 'We've done it twice already. Where will it appear?'

'It'll show up in my bathroom again. I hope I don't get into trouble – the toilet never did flush right after the *last time*.'

The next afternoon Edwin, Perpetua and Edwin's best friend Nat were walking to the science block. Nat was up to speed with what his friends were planning, and had done a bit of lateral thinking.

'Have you realised,' he said, shoving his football under one arm, 'that if you go to Hysteria, then come back and that wizard bloke rewinds time to *now*, you'll know which questions are in this test.'

Perpetua was outraged. 'Of course I've realised,' she said. 'But I don't need to resort to that sort of thing.'

Nat scoffed. 'So if you *had* to come back to now, what would be the plan, R2D2 – a memory wipe?'

'*You've* had it done plenty of times, judging by your marks!'

Edwin looked from one to the other. 'Keep your voices down! What are you two like – I don't even know if I'm going to Hysteria yet!'

Nat shot his friend a sideways glance. 'Do me a favour – I've not seen you this excited in ages.'

'It's true,' Perpetua agreed. 'Come on, Edwin, I think you've already made up your mind. I *know* you have. What's the point in delaying?'

'The point,' Edwin said firmly, 'is that I've got to hurtle through a tunnel of fire into another blimmin' parallel. We're not even talking the same universe! And all because Auvlin doesn't want to look like a loser.'

'*I'm* willing to do it,' Perpetua pointed out.

'Well good for you,' Edwin snapped. 'You just love it! Different species . . . crystals with magical power . . . another load of facts for you to remember. But it's not our world – it's not natural!'

Perpetua gave an exasperated sigh. 'But Auvlin just needs a favour – no one's been killed . . . no one's going to die.' She paused for a moment. 'I wonder . . . will you get anything in return?'

'A magic spell – like before – for anything I like.'

Nat clapped Edwin on the back. 'Maybe this time you should use it for *yourself.*'

'Oh, yes,' Perpetua trilled. 'All that hard work, and you just ended up mending Nat's broken leg. This could be a chance to do something really worthwhile!'

'Cheers,' Nat said flatly.

Edwin held up his hands. 'I know . . . I know.' He shrugged. 'We'll go, all right? Will you stop nagging me now, Perpetua?'

Perpetua squealed and kicked her heels. 'I *knew* you'd say yes!' She started walking in a tight circle. 'I've already packed, but I'll get my school notes in order before we go. You'd better take a pair of walking boots – the forest will *ruin* our trainers. Oh! And this time I'm taking some proper shampoo . . .'

That afternoon the three friends walked to Edwin's house, calling at Perpetua's on the way, where she sorted her science papers into colour-coded folders. As they turned into Grove Road, Nat and Perpetua fell silent as they noticed a man standing outside Edwin's house.

'Hello, Rownan,' Edwin said, approaching the front gate.

'Master Edwin,' Rownan said. He looked at Perpetua and Nat. 'Are these your friends?'

'Yeah. Don't worry,' Edwin replied. 'Nat won't tell *anyone*. And Perpetua has been to Hysteria already.'

Rownan nodded. 'I have heard about you,' he said to Perpetua. He looked back to Edwin. 'Have you made your decision?'

Edwin swallowed. 'Yes . . . I'm going to come back with you. And, er, Perpetua's going to join us.'

Rownan hesitated, but then said, 'Very well. Are you sure your family is not at home?'

'Positive. No one will be back for about an hour.'

Nat cleared his throat. 'I better let you go, then . . .' He held out his hand. 'Good luck, Ed.' He turned to Perpetua and gave her a nudge. 'Look after him.'

She pulled a face. 'I *was* hoping he'd look after me!'

'Well, look after each other, then.' Nat nodded to Rownan. 'Make sure they're all right, will you?' Then he coughed and turned on his heel.

Edwin and Perpetua watched Nat until he rounded the corner, then stared at each other.

'After you,' Perpetua said. 'It's *your* house.'

Edwin's heart thumped as he opened the gate and walked up the path. What was he letting himself in for? He opened the door and Perpetua and Rownan followed him in. Perpetua shut the door and crept over to Edwin, eyeing some washing on the radiator.

'Is that your underwear?' she asked. 'Are you taking any spares?'

Edwin frowned, unzipped Perpetua's rucksack and stuffed something inside. He didn't like Perpetua talking about his pants.

Rownan looked up the stairs. 'I can see the glow of the vortex at the top.'

'Oh, yes,' Perpetua whispered. 'It should be in the bathroom.'

Edwin nodded and climbed the first few steps, with Perpetua and Rownan close behind. Edwin suddenly stopped. 'D'you think there'll be enough power in the vortex to take *three* of us?'

Rownan shrugged. 'I have no knowledge of such things, Edwin.'

'Of course it'll have enough power!' Perpetua hissed. 'It took you, me and Loruis before. And anyway, did they really expect you to turn up without *me*?'

'Probably not.' Edwin blinked. He and Perpetua had made a good team last time.

From the top of the stairs they could see orange light shining through the gap around the bathroom door. A loud hum resonated around the first floor, then suddenly jumped, as if the vortex had sensed that Edwin was near.

Perpetua fumbled for Edwin's hand. 'I won't worry if you won't.'

Edwin pushed the door. As it swung back he could see a bright orange circle hovering at the other end of the bathroom, smoke swirling around its centre like storm clouds. Yellow sparks fizzed and crackled, spouting plumes of smoke.

'Rownan? Master Edwin?' a deep voice said suddenly.

Edwin jumped. 'Is that . . . *Eifus*?'

Perpetua beamed at him, nodding like mad.

'Oh, joy!' the voice cried. 'You have not forgotten us!'

'What an honour,' another, higher, voice chimed. 'We are alive and well in the memory of my bravest friend!'

'*Your* friend, dear brother? I think you will find he is on intimate terms with us both.'

'Eifus . . . Dreifus,' Rownan called. 'My time here is limited – we must hurry!'

'Of course,' Dreifus cried. 'You may both step this way!'

Edwin hesitated. 'Er, Perpetua's here, too.'

'Oh . . .' Eifus said, sounding slightly stumped. 'Was Janus expecting her?'

'He's not even expecting *me*,' Edwin said. 'You do know *all about* Auvlin's plan, don't you – that it's a secret from Janus?'

'Of course,' Eifus spluttered. 'This late addition has muddled me. We are sworn to secrecy . . . not a word will escape our lips!'

'Good.' Edwin glanced at Perpetua. 'We'd better go then . . .'

But Rownan pushed through and stepped into the vortex first. Edwin and Perpetua followed him. The heat hit their faces straight away and they were sucked in, falling through a tunnel of bright orange flame.

'Oh, God . . .' Perpetua cried. 'I'd forgotten how horrible it was!'

'I hadn't,' Edwin yelled, 'and I let *you* persuade me!'

Rownan was quite a way ahead, so Edwin and Perpetua linked arms and clung together, keeping their elbows and knees tucked in tight.

'Nearly there,' Edwin coughed as hot air seeped into his throat.

Suddenly, the flames disappeared. They were

floating in still, cold air; the only noise was a high-pitched whistle hissing in their ears.

'Remember to lie back,' Edwin said. 'Let the memories flow over you.'

After a few minutes, Perpetua murmured, 'Oh, *thank you*. I thought I'd done well, but I didn't realise . . . top of the whole borough . . . who'd have thought?'

'An A?' Edwin was whispering. 'Are you sure? . . . Yes, Mum – maybe Mr Lorius *did* like me after all . . . Anything I like? Fantastic! I'd love horse-riding lessons . . .'

Whoosh! Their memory-packed flight was over when they all landed on a huge pile of hay.

'If we could bottle that feeling, we'd make a fortune,' Perpetua said after she got her breath back. She sat up and brushed herself down.

'I wouldn't sell it,' Edwin replied. 'I'd keep it all for myself . . . I don't feel like that too often.' He brushed straw out of his hair and looked around. It was the same field as they'd landed in last time they came to Hysteria. Forest fringed the neat green grass, and the snow-topped peaks of the Balgarian Mountains rose to the north. Edwin felt his spine tingle – Emporium Castle was only a few miles away. *Janus* was only a few miles away . . .

'EDWIN! PERPETUA! How glad we are to see you!'

Eifus and Dreifus were running towards them. Eifus towered over his brother, his white candyfloss hair fluttering in the breeze. Dreifus's hands clutched at his ample waistline, his bald head gleaming in the sunshine.

'Hello, guys,' Edwin said, smiling.

'And it's very nice to see you, *too*,' Perpetua added.

Eifus bowed so deeply that when he stood up half a haystack hung from his fringe.

'Why, Lady Perpetua,' he simpered, 'it seems you have remembered our lessons in etiquette.'

'Of course!' Perpetua replied, trying not to giggle. 'You're both fine teachers.'

'Just one of our common talents,' Eifus beamed. 'You will remember, my dear – we are twins?'

Dreifus nodded. 'Identical.'

Edwin pulled Perpetua to her feet. 'Shouldn't we get out of here?'

'Step this way!' Dreifus said. 'Auvlin is waiting at Rownan's lodge. What a surprise for him to see our Lady Perpetua, too.'

Rownan led the way into the forest, and Edwin began to feel very excited. He could scarcely believe he was back in Hysteria. It almost felt like coming home. And the best thing was he could enjoy it all: he was safe. There was no threat from the Umbrians *this* time.

CHAPTER THREE

Dusk was gathering as they made their way deeper into the wood. They hadn't walked for long – no more than an hour – but Perpetua was finding the brambles and thorns hard going. At last, a wooden house came into sight. It was built of long tree trunks and its roof was made of a thick yellow thatch. A trickle of smoke slunk from the chimney, and chopped wood was stacked by the door.

'It's like something out of a fairytale,' Perpetua whispered.

'It will not be as comfortable as you are accustomed to,' Rownan said. 'But I will do my best for you and Edwin.'

'We will all make allowances, Rownan,' chimed Dreifus. 'Refinements are in short supply in the forest. For example – what use is a fish knife, when only boar and deer are plentiful?'

'Dear brother, is there such a thing as a boar knife?' Eifus asked. 'If not, perhaps we should invent one!'

They reached the lodge, and everyone followed Rownan inside. A young man who was sitting at a table stood up. He was quite tall, with long mousy hair and muddy brown eyes. He was dressed in a green tunic and long black cloak, and a silver sword hung from his brown leather belt. He was a bit older than Edwin and his hair was much longer, but they looked almost identical.

'Hello, Auvlin,' Edwin said hesitantly. The memory of this boy lying in a mausoleum, supposedly dead, was still strong in Edwin's mind. He'd seen Auvlin come to life, of course, but still . . .

'Edwin! How wonderful it is to see you! I am so glad you are willing to help me.' Auvlin strode forward and grasped Edwin's hand. 'How was your journey?'

'Er, a bit more crowded than I expected.'

'Well you are here now. Would you –' Auvlin's words fell away and he frowned. Edwin glanced backwards.

'It's Perpetua,' he said. 'You remember?'

'Oh, oh, of course. Pardon me, my lady. I did not expect you.'

'That's OK,' Perpetua muttered awkwardly.

'Er, Edwin,' Auvlin added, still looking at her curiously. 'You, you will be glad to know our friend Bellwin is here.'

Edwin glanced at Perpetua and raised his eyebrows. It hadn't even been a year – she couldn't have changed *that* much. Auvlin was more confused than he expected; no wonder he needed help with the triathlon.

'Hello, everyone,' someone said cheerfully. 'Do I hear *two* familiar voices?'

Bellwin came into the room, his round face beaming. He'd grown a little since the last time Edwin had seen him. He strode over to Edwin and grabbed his shoulder.

'It is good to see you,' he chuckled. 'I knew you would not be able to resist coming back! Would you like to see me execute a spell?' Bellwin clicked his fingers, and suddenly pungent green smoke trailed the world WOLCEME in mid-air. There was an intake of breath from his audience and Bellwin coughed and clicked his fingers again. The O and first E changed places. Edwin started to clap and Bellwin bowed, then looked up, beaming. 'And Perpetua into the bargain . . . I could not wish for more! Did Edwin have to *persuade* you to return?'

'You're kidding,' Edwin huffed. 'She had her rucksack packed before I even opened my gob!'

'That means his mouth,' Perpetua said tersely, then gave a wide smile. 'It's lovely to be back,' she said, giving Bellwin a hug. 'I thought I might come along to

29

have a look at Hysteria's wildlife. *And* I've been doing research into minerals and crystals in the last year too. So I thought, why not! There's lots I can do while Edwin is busy learning – perhaps you can help me. How are you getting on as a Full Wizard?'

'Quite well. I am even starting to help train the *new* apprentices.' He shook his head. 'Yesterday, one of them stood too close to me when practising a charm. Our spells mixed and the gatekeeper's dog, which was asleep nearby, turned into a box of frogs.' He shrugged. 'I have made one or two mistakes,' he admitted, quickly wafting the remaining green smoke away, 'but that is expected of *any* new wizard.'

'What happened to the dog?' Edwin said, slightly alarmed. He was relying on Bellwin to help him get through this visit to Hysteria, after all.

'We reversed the spell and got him back,' Bellwin said breezily. 'Although one of the frogs had hopped away, so the dog was a little shorter in the leg than before.'

There was an awkward silence.

Perpetua crossed her arms. 'Bellwin, *why* are you doing this magic for Auvlin?' she demanded. 'If Ollwin or Janus knew, you'd be in *all sorts* of trouble.'

'Neither my father nor Ollwin will find out,' Auvlin said. He shot Perpetua a hard look. 'As long as my plan is kept secret.'

Perpetua stared back, indignant.

Edwin went to say something, but Dreifus bleated, 'To save the king from worry is an honourable aim, and we are *all* proud to assist our young prince to victory. Auvlin will recover his full senses in time, and a helping hand to win the triathlon will harm no one.'

Edwin gave Perpetua an encouraging smile, then looked at Rownan. 'Well, as you're going to be my teacher, you'd better tell me all about it!'

Eifus waggled a finger in the air. 'Refreshments first! We have prepared a stew from our dear departed mother's recipe book, using the yields of the forest.' He scuttled to the fire and took a ladle from a bubbling pot. 'Cockroach dumplings, anyone?'

They'd finished their meal, and Eifus eyed Edwin and Perpetua's plates.

'Are our dumplings not to your taste, my young friends?'

'I, er . . . had bugs last night for dinner,' Edwin replied. 'You know what they say – everything in moderation.'

'Do they?' Eifus switched his stare. 'And you, my lady?'

'I had dinner with Edwin,' she said quickly. 'And he's right . . . you can have too much of a good thing.'

'Ah, well . . .' Eifus spooned four speckled lumps from each of their plates. 'Mother would say we should not waste such delicious fare.' He grinned at Perpetua. 'Of course, being such magnificent physical specimens my brother and I can afford to over-indulge every now and then.' He took a crunchy bite then made a face. 'Dreifus – perhaps next time we should discard the cockroach shells before cooking.'

Once everything had been cleared away they all huddled around the table with large mugs of hot, sweet milk.

'Can I ask you something, Auvlin?' Perpetua said.

'Yes, of course.' The prince seemed a little more relaxed now.

'Do you remember anything of when you were in the mausoleum – when everyone thought you were dead?'

Auvlin shook his head. 'Nothing.' He sighed. 'It is still hard to believe the Umbrians tried to pass the soul of their wretched king into my body. They wanted to see Ancient Magical Lore abandoned to rule Hysteria and Umbria as one.'

'Yes,' Bellwin said gravely. 'It is fortunate that the worst elements of Shadow Magic – the movement of souls and transformation – require so much time and power. If Umbria's mines yielded more crystals, we would surely be in much greater danger.'

'Shadow Magic must always be resisted,' Auvlin said. 'When I lay still and cold in the mausoleum, Ollwin could have sought to use it to transform any

Hysterian to take my place. But *that* would have broken Ancient Magical Lore. He and my father did right – they brought Edwin here.'

Eifus clapped his hands. 'That, to my mind, is the greatest decision Janus has ever made! I have already advised the king that we should designate an *Edwin's Day*.' He beamed. 'Jousting, feasting . . . a *Best Earthling* challenge.' He glanced at Perpetua. 'We would honour you too, my lady. Perhaps a pin-the-tail-on-the-hog . . . for the little ones.'

Perpetua sat stonily silent as Edwin smothered a smirk. 'So this competition, Auvlin – it's orienteering, right?'

'Yes, I am now returned to full strength, but for some reason I cannot find my way around Hysteria as well as before.'

Perpetua sat forward. 'You know, it's not at all surprising.' She held up a hand and pincered her finger and thumb. 'Being that close to death must have an almost catastrophic effect. It's –'

'Yeah. Whatever!' Edwin barked.

Perpetua blinked and the others looked startled. 'He's, er . . . he's telling me to be quiet,' she explained.

Auvlin seemed keen to change the subject back to the race. 'Not long ago, Perpetua, my father sent me to a wizard for treatment. I needed to rediscover my memories of the kingdom over which I will eventually rule. His magic *seemed* to work at first, but on the journey back to Hysteria my improvement dwindled away. My father was so sure I would be cured, I could not – and *cannot* – bring myself to tell him the truth.'

'So I'm part of the cover-up,' Edwin said, a little uncomfortably. 'Everyone will think *you're* competing in this triathlon, and Janus won't be any the wiser.'

'Yes. Hysterian princes have taken part for centuries, and very few have lost. This one is being held in Hysteria for the honour of the Janus line – I *must* win.'

Edwin blinked. 'Well, at least you'll have a home advantage.'

'He means you'll have the most supporters,' Perpetua said quickly. She leant towards Auvlin. 'Wouldn't your father understand that you're not quite back to normal, after all you've been through?'

'He must *not* know,' Auvlin said briskly, almost rising from his seat. 'His health was ravaged by what happened to me. He is still frail and I will not expose him to more anxiety!'

Perpetua held up her hands. 'OK . . . It was only a thought.'

In the brief silence that followed, Edwin swallowed a mouthful of milk. He hoped Janus was all right. 'Let's get back to the orienteering competition,' he said. 'How long does it last?'

'A day,' Auvlin replied. 'Rownan will spend the next week teaching you about the terrain – he knows it very well. I will come here as often as I can, when my father does not need me. I hope to regain some of my memory by sitting with you during your lessons.'

'Can I have a quick look at the maps *now*?' Edwin said eagerly.

'Of course.' Rownan disappeared into another room.

Perpetua looked at Bellwin. 'Does he live here on his own?'

'Rownan has a son called Mornan,' Bellwin whispered. 'I have only seen him a few times, working with his father. He is an odd fellow – I merely said hello once, and he started with fright.'

Rownan's return stopped that particular conversation. He unfolded a large map on the table and sat down beside Edwin.

'The trial will cover this part of Hysteria,' he began. He drew a line with his finger. 'The area is mainly within the Inigo Forest here, but it extends to the Leigh River in the west. It is very good for orienteering.'

'And do you use a map and compass, like we do at home?' Edwin asked hopefully.

'Yes,' Rownan replied, adding, 'We have no magical tools for these tasks.'

'Great,' Edwin said. 'I'm actually really looking forward to it!'

'Do not forget the crystal mines!' a voice boomed from above, scaring the life out of Edwin. Everyone looked up.

'Yes, Mornan, I *had* remembered,' Rownan replied, as if it were perfectly normal to respond to a disembodied voice. He pulled the map towards him and picked up a quill. 'There are two crystal mines in the territory – here and here. All competitors will be warned.'

Edwin's eyes narrowed. 'Warned about what?'

'That they must not be entered,' came the voice from above.

'The mines are very dangerous,' Rownan said, looking straight at Edwin. 'Only Janus, Auvlin and those who work there may enter them – others who do so put themselves in *great* danger.'

Edwin frowned. 'But . . . but I haven't got to go *underground* have I?' Suddenly he was feeling a bit hot and bothered.

'No, but some clues to the trail may be buried. You must be certain of where the crystal mines are.' He scratched his quill deeper into the map. 'Do not worry – I will make sure you are well taught.'

'That's all right then,' Edwin said folding his arms, not at all sure that is *was*.

'My friend, do I detect a little *anxiety*?' asked Dreifus carefully.

'Too right!' Edwin snapped. 'The last time I came here, Janus promised I'd be safe – then I ended up going to war and nearly got myself executed!' He glared at Perpetua. 'Why did I let you talk me into coming back?'

'Because you knew there'd be no danger this time,' she said as if she were talking to a toddler. 'All you've got to do is concentrate on your studies and avoid those crystal mines.'

'It's as simple as that, is it? Why don't *you* do the trial, then?'

'Because – funnily enough – I don't look like a prince!'

Auvlin grabbed Edwin's arm. 'I beg you, do not change your mind. I promise you will come to no harm. Do you think my father would let me compete in the trial if *my* life were at risk?'

Edwin leant back a little. Auvlin needed to chill out. 'I s'pose not,' he said. He turned to Rownan. 'Are the entrances to these mines really obvious? Would I have to be really stupid to get myself inside one?'

'I know where to find them – I will show you myself.'

'Did you work in the mines?' Perpetua asked Rownan.

He stood up. 'Not *me*, my lady . . .' Rownan mumbled. 'Now, I must bid you goodnight.' He hurriedly folded the map and disappeared upstairs.

'Is he OK?' Edwin said softly.

'Oh, yes,' Bellwin replied. 'I am sure there is nothing wrong.'

'And that voice – that *was* his son?'

Bellwin nodded, and whispered, 'I told you . . . he is an odd fellow.'

Auvlin and Bellwin decided they should make their way back to the castle before nightfall. Eifus and Dreifus set off too, promising they'd be back bright and early to help Edwin and Perpetua settle in.

Edwin and Perpetua were sleeping downstairs in the lodge. They were quite relieved as Mornan hadn't sounded like a bundle of laughs. Edwin chucked his bedding on his bunk then watched Perpetua carefully arrange her covers. She glanced at him.

'You're quiet – what's the matter?'

'I've been thinking about what you said before we came – that there'd be no danger this time.' Edwin huffed. 'It's all right for you. While I'm skirting round land mines you'll be floating around the forest like David Attenborough!'

'Don't be such a drama queen,' Perpetua told him, getting into bed. 'Rownan said he'll make sure you don't get into any trouble.'

'I hope so.' Edwin flopped down onto his feather mattress. 'I'm whacked. That vortex really takes it out of you.'

'Yes . . . I'd forgotten what it was like.' Perpetua folded her arms behind her head. 'But then I think mainly about the good things from Hysteria. Maybe my subconscious tries to block out the scary bits. Like the Umbrians and all that stuff they do . . . passing souls into different bodies, transforming people to look like someone else. It's so gruesome!'

Edwin frowned into the darkness. 'We know from last time that Shadow Magic turns whoever uses it into a vampire. But how d'you reckon it changes them physically?'

'I don't know. And no one in Hysteria would be able to tell us, so I'm not alone. Remember what Ollwin said – they know very little about Shadow Magic here.' Perpetua yawned. 'I wonder if people at home think we've run away together?'

'Maybe,' Edwin replied. 'Everyone knows we're friends now.'

'On second thoughts, I don't think so,' Perpetua added. 'They all know I'm far too clever for you.'

Edwin heard Perpetua give what sounded like a contented sigh. He rolled over, closed his eyes and started to think about Janus. His mental image of the king had become a little bit fuzzy in the time he'd been away. But while he was here, was there a chance Edwin might visit Emporium Castle again?

Chapter Four

The next morning Edwin was woken by the clunk of a door. He looked over at Perpetua. Her eyes were closed, but she was stirring.

Edwin yawned as he tiptoed to a window, pulling the rough curtain aside. He blinked against the dappled light and focused on two figures setting off on a path into the forest. One was unmistakably Rownan; the other man had a similar build and the same colour hair. It must be Mornan.

'What are you doing?'

Edwin looked around. Perpetua had propped herself up on an elbow.

'Nothing. I was just watching Rownan and his son

walk into the wood.'

'What does he look like? Mornan, I mean.'

'I only saw the back of his head. But I could see what Bellwin meant when he said he was odd. He looked young and quite strong, but he seemed very careful about where he was walking.'

Perpetua stretched then swung her legs over the side of her bed. 'Have they left us anything to eat?'

They went to the fireplace to investigate. The cooking pot was empty and all the bowls and plates were clean. There wasn't even a piece of bread lying around.

'Great,' Perpetua moaned, pulling a cardigan from her rucksack. 'At least they fed us when we were at the castle.'

'We won't get five-star treatment here,' Edwin said flatly. 'We're roughing it now, you know. Maybe we should've eaten those cockroaches last night . . .' He glanced around the room. 'Where else can we look?'

'There,' Perpetua said, pointing upwards.

'Where laughing boy lives? It's worth a try, I suppose.'

Edwin went first, carefully scaling the narrow wooden steps. He popped his head into the first floor room and looked around. Two beds were positioned at either end of the room (one a double, the other a single). There was a chair beside each, and two cupboards sat in between. Edwin took the final steps then pulled up Perpetua.

'Shall we look in those?' he said, nodding to the cupboards. But they were filled with hats, leggings, thick woollen coats and rough grey tunics.

'There's nowhere else here they could store food,' Peretua sighed. 'I think we're going to have to wait until they get back.' She looked around the room and fixed her gaze on something.

'Hey – what's that . . . ?' Perpetua scuttled to the chair by the single bed. A small book lay on the covers; a sliver of paper between its open leaves, and more poking out from other pages. Perpetua picked up the book and pulled her glasses from her cardigan pocket. '"The Armegia Charm",' she read, creasing her nose.

'The Armegia what?' Edwin asked.

Perpetua prodded a finger at a line drawing. 'This must be it. There's a description. "A relic from the Eastern Lands. A yellow Balgarian crystal cast in metallic Jura. Made in Meticulla. Properties unknown".'

Edwin leant over Perpetua's shoulder. The drawing showed something that looked like a brass oval with a whopping great crystal in the centre. 'What's on the other pages?' he said.

Perpetua flicked to the next paper bookmark.

'"The Niosin Amulet",' Edwin read. '"Grey flatweave stone on a twisted silver chain. Made in Hysteria. Properties unknown".'

Perpetua flicked on again. '"The Dervin Crystalmass. Six white crystals set in a yellow-gold sphere. Made in

Oreon. Properties unknown".' She frowned, then opened up all the marked pages one by one. 'Everything that's been singled out all say the same – *properties unknown*. What does that mean? What *are* they?'

Edwin flipped over the book's cover. 'Why don't you try looking at the title? There you are – *Ancient Relics of These Territories.*' He was delighted with himself.

Perpetua opened the book again, and ran her fingertips over a page border. 'And what are these patterns?' she said. 'They're all the way through.'

'The Hysterians don't need an excuse to go over the top – everything's got a flounce or a flourish! Except this place.' Edwin looked around. 'Is this what Mornan does with his time up here, then – reading about shiny stones and bits of jewellery?' But Edwin suddenly felt uneasy. 'You'd better put that back as it was – we don't want Rownan to know we've been looking through their stuff.'

Perpetua slapped the book back down on the bed. Edwin had forgotten how grumpy she could be when she was hungry. 'Perhaps they should've left us some breakfast then,' she said tartly. 'Do they expect us to survive on fresh air?'

Thankfully, Eifus and Dreifus came to the rescue twenty minutes later. Perpetua was combing her hair as they bustled through the door with Bellwin not far behind.

'Ah!' Drefius beamed, heaving a bag up onto the

table, which wasn't much lower than him. 'I see you are doing your ablutions. Very wise – the one who does not brush her hair today will look like a vagrant tomorrow.'

Bellwin giggled and Perpetua smiled through gritted teeth. 'Have you brought us anything to eat?'

'Oh, yes!' Eifus replied eagerly, flicking back his long white hair. 'As ever, your comfort is our highest priority. Service is our very watch word.'

'Bread!' Dreifus said with a flourish, and produced a large brown loaf.

'And soft cheese,' Eifus added, looking down at Dreifus. 'An ideal accompaniment. They go together like . . . like . . .'

'Like Eifus and Dreifus!' Dreifus cried.

'Of course, dear brother. Why did I not think of that?'

'Because, brother dear,' Dreifus said lightly. 'Our dear departed mother always said my wits were a little faster than yours.'

'She did not!' Eifus blinked; he was obviously thinking hard. 'She said . . . she said your *nits* were faster than mine! Why, they were often seen racing from one strand of your hair to the other.'

Dreifus clamped his lips and picked up a bread knife. He eyed his brother as he cut the first slice, then slammed a slab of cheese on top.

'There,' he grunted, throwing it at Perpetua. '*Milk*, my lady?'

'Er . . . yes please,' she squeaked, trying not to annoy anyone.

Edwin waited for his breakfast to be served then sat down at the table. 'Let's make this a nice calm start to the day,' he said. 'Where's Auvlin this morning?'

'He is busy with something at the castle,' Bellwin replied, sitting next to Edwin. 'How did you find him yesterday?'

'We thought he was a bit confused,' Perpetua butted in. '*Is it* just his sense of direction that's been effected?'

'Yes, as far as I know,' Bellwin replied.

'I was wondering about that,' Edwin said. 'How is Auvlin going to get on when I go home – surely he'll still need to find his way around Hysteria?'

'I went back to the wizard who treated Auvlin,' Bellwin replied. 'He admitted the magic could sometimes, although rarely, wane – but he predicts it will gain strength, and Auvlin will regain his sense of direction. And can you guess who the wizard is?'Bellwin grinned. 'Hildeguard Brolin – the very one we visited after the Cave of Spells!'

'I won't forget *him* in a hurry,' Perpetua laughed.

'But Ollwin seemed to think Brolin was really good,' Edwin said. 'Wouldn't you have expected *his* magic to work properly?'

'Yes, indeed,' Bellwin sighed. 'Brolin *himself* was very anxious – and astonished – when I told him what had happened, as he had given Auvlin his word that he would be cured. But, as I said, he was confident his sense of direction would eventually come back to him.'

Eifus sniffed. 'I understand Wizard Brolin never washes his hair. Just imagine! We are all aware that he helped us against the Umbrians, but a wizard should never lose sight of his ablutions.'

'I could not agree more, brother dear,' Dreifus trilled. 'As our dear departed mother would say, the one who does not wash his armpits is the one who will remain friendless.'

Eifus beamed. 'We have many friends, dear brother.'

'Yes . . . and *very* clean armpits.'

Edwin and Perpetua giggled.

'Now, brother dear,' Dreifus said, getting up. 'Let us go into the forest to find something for *our* breakfast.' The twins scurried outside.

'How are you both this morning?' Bellwin said.

'Better for this.' Perpetua held her mug aloft. 'Rownan and his son aren't here. Edwin saw them earlier this morning, walking into the forest.'

'They are probably hunting for this evening's meal,' Bellwin said. 'No doubt a nice rabbit stew . . . or venison. Did you meet Mornan, Edwin?'

'No, I only got a glimpse of him. But can I ask you about something? We went upstairs to look for some food, and we found a book with loads of strange drawings in it. It was –'

'It was called *Ancient Relics of These Territories*,' Perpetua interrupted.

Edwin blinked. 'Someone had marked quite a few pages in it . . . and they all said the same thing about the stuff they showed – *properties unknown*.'

'I know the book,' Bellwin replied. 'There is a copy in the castle library that I had to read during my apprenticeship. It lists all the ancient relics that exist in these territories. They were all made for a purpose and have been charmed in some way to perform a task – for example, to ensure that water is safe to drink, or perhaps protect something that is precious . . .' Bellwin linked his fingers. 'But some relics are so old their purpose is not known. Hence, *properties unknown*.'

'Right,' Edwin said slowly. 'D'you know anyone who's got one?'

'Oh, yes. The family of Janus has two or three, owned for many centuries, since they came to rule Hysteria. Although I do not know how they are used as only King Janus and a few others are privy to that.'

Edwin frowned. That sounded interesting, but something didn't make sense. 'Bellwin, last night, did you say that Mornan *worked* with Rownan?'

'Yes, as far as I know he helps his father in the forest from time to time. I believe he did some other kind of work years ago – but what I do not know.'

'So why would Rownan or Mornan be interested in old charms?' Edwin asked. 'Wouldn't that be more for someone like *you* – for a wizard?'

Bellwin smiled. 'Yes, but for anyone else it could be a hobby . . . a matter of interest.'

Edwin swallowed a mouthful of milk. That'd be the same as his parents – they were always banging on about the World Wars and the British Empire, but they were certainly never soldiers.

'So,' Edwin said. 'How's things at the castle?'

'Not very good,' Bellwin admitted.

'Janus isn't onto us?' Perpetua asked quickly.

'No, Auvlin's plan is quite safe. *I* am the one in trouble.'

'Oh, dear . . . what've you done?'

Bellwin bit his lip. 'I used quite a lot of power bringing you here, and I did not want Ollwin to suspect my actions. So I prepared three crystals in one go, instead of the usual two, and put them in the vortex. The power level rose, as I wanted, but the auras mixed too quickly, making the most terrible stench . . .' He shook his head, but half-smiled. 'The throne room smells like a bad goose egg! Ollwin suspects nothing, but the stench has made him ever more bad tempered.'

'Well, he can be a right misery! What's wrong with him *now*?' Edwin asked.

'Ever since you left Hysteria, the Umbrians have been preying on Ollwin's mind. They came so close to killing our royal family, and he is worried they may try again. Hysteria's safety is his deepest concern.'

48

'But it's like you told us,' Perpetua said. 'The Umbrians don't have many crystals, so they can't perform much Shadow Magic unless they get more from elsewhere.' Her eyes narrowed. 'I take it that's why Hysteria's crystal mines are heavily guarded – to keep the Umbrians and others out?'

'Yes,' Bellwin replied. 'They are overseen by a presence unknown to all but King Janus. It was acquired by Janus the tenth, and the secret has been passed down through all his descendents to our present Janus the eighty-third. In each king's lifetime, there are only a few who know how this mysterious guardian works.' He blinked. 'Except, of course, those who have been confronted by it. But it is said their encounter would not leave them in any condition to tell the tale.'

'What d'you mean?' Edwin asked.

'The injuries inflicted leave them too shocked to speak properly . . . and they die soon after.'

'Crikey,' Perpetua groaned. 'That sounds horrible.' She frowned. 'I assume they need miners to *work* in these mines . . .'

Bellwin nodded. 'The crystals do not dig themselves out,' he said, smiling. 'As far as I know, the miners go through a secret ritual before they start their first day's work – as a result the guardian presence knows they are permitted to enter the mines, and it will not harm them.'

'So once it's done, this presence thing will always recognise the miners?' Edwin said. 'Like, forever?'

'No, the ritual is renewed twice a year, inside Emporium Castle.'

'And what about Janus and Auvlin – Rownan said they went into the mines, too.'

'I have heard that because they are from the Janus line they only need go through the ceremony once in their lifetime.'

Voices floated in from outside. Rownan came in, and Edwin and Perpetua stood up. Mornan strode to the wooden steps and quickly climbed them, his gaze lowered, although Edwin caught a glimpse of his long, pale face.

'Morning,' Edwin said flatly as he watch him disappear. He turned to Rownan and frowned. 'Your son doesn't seem too happy that we're here.'

Rownan threw three dead rabbits on the table, a muscle twitching in his cheek. 'We should look at the maps again this morning. I will bring them. Please be seated, Edwin.'

Bellwin and Perpetua had already wandered into the forest on a fact-finding mission when Edwin's lesson began. First Edwin was shown how to use a Hysterian compass, then Rownan brought out a map of land that included Emporium Castle. Edwin learned about the map's symbols, then he and Rownan followed a simple trail from the castle through the forest to the position of the lodge. Even though Edwin paid close attention, his gaze sometimes strayed when he heard the floorboards above him creak.

After a couple of hours Edwin asked for a break. He got up and stretched his legs, then walked outside. Eifus and Dreifus were skipping through a sea of flowers in a nearby meadow, crying out with delight as they picked an occasional bloom.

'This one, dear brother, will be for Merrymaid. She fluttered her eyelashes at me last evening – there was no mistake.'

'And *this one*, brother dear, will be for Heffalumpia. She gave me an extra ladle of porridge this morning. When my undergarments strained against my stomach, I knew!'

Edwin laughed so much he almost didn't notice Perpetua and Bellwin walking towards him.

'Have you heard these two?' he guffawed. 'They're bonkers!'

'I think we know that already,' Perpetua said quickly. 'Bellwin and I have something to tell you, don't we, Bellwin?'

'Yes, we do.'

'We've been talking about it – haven't we, Bellwin?'

'Yes, we have.'

'And we came to a decision, didn't we, Bellwin?'

'Yes, we –'

'Come over here, Edwin. Bellwin will explain.'

'If he can get a word in edgeways,' Edwin mumbled as they trudged towards some trees. Perpetua sat down and crossed her legs. Bellwin slumped down with his chin on his knees and Edwin sat between his two friends.

'So?' he said.

'We decided that Bellwin needs to get back in Ollwin's good books.'

Edwin looked straight at Bellwin. '*Did* you? Really?'

Bellwin nodded meekly. 'Yes . . . I did.'

Edwin glanced at Perpetua. 'You can't let her boss you around, you know. She tries it with me at school, but I don't have any of it.'

'I do not! I've got better things to think about at school than *you*, thank you very much.'

Edwin waved the suggestion away. 'Whatever. So, Bellwin – what's the plan?'

Perpetua opened her mouth to explain, but Edwin silenced her with a look.

'We . . . er, I decided,' Bellwin began uncertainly, 'that I should investigate Shadow Magic.'

Edwin pulled a face. 'Shadow Magic? The cause of all the wars between Hysteria and Umbria – is that such a good idea?'

'I will not *practise* the art,' Bellwin assured him hurriedly, 'but merely try to find out more about it.'

'And how are you going to do that? I thought no one here was allowed to study Shadow Magic.' He remembered thinking this was odd the last time he was here.

'Not, in Hysteria, no . . .'

Edwin sat up. 'You're not gonna go to Umbria?'

'Of course not!' Perpetua hissed. 'Honestly! How stupid do you think he is?'

Bellwin didn't flinch. 'I could go to Meticulla,' he whispered. 'To Hildeguard Brolin.'

Edwin's mouth gapped. '*He* doesn't practise . . . ?'

'Oh, no,' Bellwin said quickly. 'But he has read about it for many years, purely out of interest. When I took Auvlin to see him we had a very enlightening conversation – just us two . . . wizard to wizard.'

'I see,' Edwin said slowly. 'But how *exactly* will this get you into Ollwin's good books?'

'He would dearly love Janus to defeat the Umbrians once and for all. But to do this, we need to know much more about how Shadow Magic works.' Bellwin's eyes glinted. 'If I can find out something – anything – of importance, we may see a way to end the Umbrian threat.'

'And Brolin can teach you this stuff?'

'He has written down everything he knows. He has shelves and shelves of notebooks and there is yet more to be discovered.'

'Right. And when are you planning to do this?'

'As soon as I can,' Bellwin said brightly. 'Perhaps you and Perpetua would like to come, too?'

'Could we, Edwin?' Perpetua said eagerly. 'We were talking about Shadow Magic only last night . . . wondering how it worked and all that.'

Bellwin looked horrified, and she patted his arm gently. 'Just curiosity,' she soothed him. 'It's difficult not to wonder.'

'What?' Edwin slapped his forehead with the heel of his hand. 'Having a chat at bedtime is one thing. Handling dangerous information like that is something else.' He leant closer to Perpetua. 'Don't you remember the last time we were here – Janus asked me to go to war, and *you* told him we hadn't come to Hysteria for *that*. Now listen to you – deciding we should get involved in exactly the same things that nearly got us killed! Anyway, we haven't got time. I've got to learn all this stuff, then the orienteering will start.'

For once, Perpetua shut up. But it was only when Edwin noticed her staring past him that he realised why – Auvlin was approaching the lodge.

Bellwin stood up. 'I thought you were helping your father today, Auvlin?'

'I changed my mind,' Auvlin replied. He looked at Edwin. 'How were this morning's lessons?'

'OK . . .' Edwin was slightly cagey. 'Still a lot to learn, though.'

'But you feel you will be able to compete?'

'Yeah. No problem.'

'Excellent.' Auvlin fiddled with his belt. 'You *will*

54

spend all your time studying for the trial?' He glanced at Bellwin. 'You will not be distracted?'

'I don't plan to do anything else,' Edwin replied flatly.

Auvlin gave what looked like a relieved smile. 'That seems wise. There is not much else in Hysteria to provide amusement. Can you demonstrate what you have learnt this morning? I am keen to see your progress.'

'Yeah, OK . . . gimme a minute.'

Auvlin nodded, turned and walked back to the lodge.

'What's his problem?' Edwin whispered to Bellwin and Perpetua. 'If I'd known he'd be *this* pushy I wouldn't have bothered. I'm doing him a favour!' He sighed and followed the prince.

'Now, Bellwin,' Perpetua said when she was sure she was out of earshot. 'How long would it take us to get to Meticulla?'

CHAPTER FIVE

Three days later, Perpetua was still banging on about Shadow Magic. Bellwin got the brunt of it as Edwin had been studying hard with Rownan.

Edwin and Perpetua still hadn't met Mornan, and Edwin was starting to wonder if he was avoiding them; perhaps he should've packed some deodorant after all.

Auvlin and Bellwin came to the lodge for dinner, and Rownan told everyone that he and Mornan had to go away for a few days. He suggested that Edwin use the time to practise the orienteering skills he'd learnt.

'Great!' Edwin said. 'I can't wait to get out there.'

'There is something I must do before that,' Bellwin

said. 'Perform the maturing charm. You must look *just like* Auvlin again – no half measures will do.'

'And when you go out I must stay inside,' Auvlin added. 'We cannot risk us *both* being seen at the same time.'

Edwin felt quite excited. The last time the Maturing Charm had been used, he'd gone from twelve years old to fourteen in a matter of seconds. What would he look like *this time*, at fifteen?

'Come on then,' he said briskly, 'let's get on with it!'

Bellwin and Edwin stood in front of the fireplace. Edwin's fingers wrestled nervously; he knew the process didn't hurt, but it wasn't exactly pleasant.

'It is a shame we cannot use the Spirit Dungeon,' Bellwin sighed. 'But Rownan's lodge will just have to do.' He raised his hand and his palm began to glow, then white light flickered between his fingers. 'Look up,' he instructed.

Edwin's gaze wandered to the wooden ceiling and his eyes widened. There was a gap in the boards, and he could see an ear pressed to the upstairs floor. Wouldn't it be more interesting for Mornan to *look* at what was happening?

He jumped when Bellwin suddenly yelled, 'Can-tan-te agerium velixia!'

An arc of electricity flashed from the wizard's fingers towards Edwin's temples. He jolted upwards, and his body floated inches above the ground.

'Can-tan-te agerium momentia!'

An icy tingle rippled across Edwin's skin. He let air trickle from his chest, and he tried to say, 'Ugh, I remember this . . .' but the words were muffled.

'Can-tan-te agerium finalia!'

Edwin's skin grew warmer. He was slowly lowered down, and the feeling came back into his arms and legs. He flopped into a chair, shivering.

'Oh, Bellwin,' cooed Perpetua, 'you're so much more masterful now!'

Bellwin blushed.

Edwin scraped long brown locks back from his face. 'How's my voice?' He laughed. 'Wow . . . that sounds a lot better.' He stood up. 'How much taller am I than last time?'

'At *least* three millimetres,' Perpetua sniffed.

'You're just jealous,' Edwin said. 'You'd *love* to know what you're going to look like in two years' time.' He folded his arms. '*I* can tell you – a few inches taller, a lot more spots and the same geeky glasses.'

Perpetua folded her arms. 'I'll have you know my mother has my eyes tested annually! So it'll be *new* geeky glasses by then.'

Rownan stood up. 'I am afraid we do not have a mirror here, Edwin – you cannot look at your reflection.'

'Yes he can, Rownan.' Suddenly Auvlin was by his side, grasping Edwin's arm. 'You need only look at me.'

Edwin and Auvlin gazed at each other, and Edwin remembered exactly how he looked as a Hysterian prince – muddy-brown eyes a little deeper set, his jaw more square; long brown locks flowing to his shoulders. Edwin smiled and now, suddenly, Auvlin looked at ease.

'You could be twins!' Eifus announced.

'Identical!' Dreifus cried. 'Just like us!'

Perpetua giggled, and Edwin turned to Rownan. 'It's a few hours from getting dark – can I go out into the forest now, just for a little while?'

'Of course,' Rownan replied. 'But do not go alone.'

'*You* cannot help him, Father,' a voice came from above. 'You must attend to me.'

Bellwin said he had some reading to do. Eifus and Dreifus looked at Edwin and hopped up and down hopefully. He pulled a face and turned to Perpetua.

'Fancy a turn around the forest?'

'Why not,' Perpetua replied. She pointed at Edwin's feet. 'But don't you think you'd better get changed first?'

Edwin looked down. His trousers were now at least six centimetres too short. Pah! So much for Perpetua's three millimetres!

'Come on, Perpetua – this way!'

Perpetua was rattling around in the undergrowth,

looking for the lesser-spotted whatsistname. 'All right!' she moaned. 'This isn't all about *you*, you know!'

Edwin peered at his map in the early evening light, then set his compass to north north-west. He grinned – he was really getting to grips with these instruments. 'I said *this way* . . .'

'Haven't we been up there already?' Perpetua whined as she fought her way out of the bushes.

'Yes – but from the other direction,' Edwin said. 'Don't you know *anything*?'

'I know plenty more than you!'

'Yeah, right – really useful stuff like the square route of a zillion billion. But you've got no sense of direction!'

Perpetua seemed to know Edwin was right, because she quickly changed the subject. 'Mornan's a funny one, isn't he?'

Edwin scoffed. 'Understatement of the year. He's plain weird!'

'Where d'you think they're going tomorrow?'

'No idea. And there's no way they're going to tell us. It's not a problem though, is it? We can –'

'We can go to Meticulla!' Perpetua trilled as if she'd just realised it. 'Bellwin says he can get us some horses. Come on, we love riding!' She put her hands together. 'Please, Edwin, *please*.'

'I don't know,' Edwin muttered.

'But what's the use of navigating to any old place, just to turn around and come straight back again?

All right for you, but *so* boring for the rest of us.'

'It's called *practice*, Perpetua.' Edwin had adopted the same tone of voice that she usually used for him.

'Yes, but we can travel to Meticulla with a *purpose*. Bellwin's sure Brolin can teach us lots about Shadow Magic – and if that helps Hysteria in the long run, so much the better. You'd be helping Janus.'

Edwin sighed and tucked his map under his arm. Why did Perpetua have an answer for *everything*? 'Come on,' he grunted. 'Let's go back to the lodge.'

Perpetua grinned and picked her way through some foliage. 'Whatever you say . . .'

After ten minutes of striding through the forest Edwin hadn't said another word, and Perpetua was still hanging back. But she caught up when Edwin came to an abrupt halt.

'Stop!' he whispered, raising his hand. 'Someone's there . . .'

They sidled behind a tree. In the middle distance three mounted horses were plodding through a sea of bracken; the horse at the back was led by a rope, and the boy riding it wore what looked like a metal helmet that covered his face. A man and a woman rode the other horses, scouring the forest around them.

'Are they lost?' Perpetua whispered.

'Not sure – either that or they don't wanna be seen.'

'Hurry!' the woman growled, making Edwin and Perpetua shrink back. 'Kick your horse!'

The boy held up his hands; they were bound together. 'I cannot keep my balance,' came his muffled reply. 'And I need to drink . . .'

The woman grunted and swung her horse round. Taking a bottle from her saddle bag, she opened it and thrust it between the boy's hands. She looked carefully about her, but Edwin and Perpetua were well hidden in the evening shadows. The woman pulled the helmet from the boy's head.

Edwin's eyes narrowed and Perpetua leant forward. They could only see the boy from the back and it was quite a distance, but . . .

'He looks a bit like Auvlin!' Edwin took a step forward. 'Don't you think?'

Perpetua pulled Edwin back. 'They might see you!' She shrugged. 'I can't see as well as you. But yes, I know what you mean.'

The boy lowered the bottle and the woman snatched it back. She jammed the boy's helmet back on and turned to lead the horses through the forest again.

'That couldn't have been Auvlin, could it?' Edwin said as they disappeared from sight.

'Of course not!' Perpetua snapped. 'He said he'd make sure he'd stay inside while you were out. And anyway, those people didn't look the sort that royalty hang around with.'

'Yeah, course.' Edwin frowned. 'D'you reckon the boy was some sort of prisoner?'

'It looked like he was being taken somewhere – perhaps it was to jail?'

Edwin scratched his head. 'Do they have prisons and stuff in Hysteria?'

'Why wouldn't they?' Perpetua said. 'They can't all be like Janus and Ollwin – every nation has its bad apples.'

Edwin glanced uncomfortably around the forest. 'Come on,' he muttered. 'Let's get a move on – and *this time*, keep up!'

Edwin and Perpetua got back to the lodge not long before dark. They found Bellwin huddled over a book and Auvlin asleep by the fire.

'Have you two been waiting for us all this time?' Edwin asked Bellwin.

'Oh, yes – we have been talking about the last time you came to Hysteria!'

Edwin looked at Perpetua. She nodded and jerked her head towards the door.

'Come outside,' she mouthed at Bellwin.

Once they were all out of the lodge, Perpetua wasted no time.

'I suggested to Edwin that we go to Meticulla tomorrow, while Rownan is away. You told me we can get there in a day – we can spend an evening talking about Shadow Magic with Brolin, then we can come back the *following* day. It's the perfect opportunity!'

'We could, but *no one* else must know.'

'That's easy – you can think of something to tell Rownan and Auvlin!'

Bellwin thought for a moment. 'I have an uncle and aunt in Meticulla. I could say I am visiting them.'

'That sounds perfect! What time could we make a start?'

Bellwin thought for a moment. 'Rownan and Mornan are leaving at first light – if we leave not long after we will arrive in Meticulla before dark.' He looked at Edwin. 'Do you think your navigation skills are good enough? Did you find your way in the forest?'

'Yeah, I was really –'

'Oh, we saw some people riding in the forest, Bellwin,' Perpetua interrupted. 'They were quite far away, but one of them looked a bit like Auvlin.'

'Did he?' Bellwin frowned. 'In what way?'

'We only saw the back of his head,' Edwin replied. 'But the hair looked a lot like his. He just *reminded* me of Auvlin, that's all.'

Bellwin smiled. 'Since his return to health, many young men have copied how he looks. Unfortunately my hair is too thin to suit a longer style.'

Edwin was just about to mention that the boy seemed to be a prisoner, when Perpetua cut in.

'Right, back to Meticulla. Bellwin – you can bring

some supplies for the journey in the morning, and anything else you think we might need. No stewed cockroaches, though. Edwin – I suggest you study the route tonight and make a list of landmarks that you can tick off along the way. You should also double-check the distance we have to travel.'

Edwin stared at Perpetua, shaking his head. 'You've got to be the *bossiest* person I've ever met . . .'

Perpetua smiled at Bellwin. 'He means I like telling people what to do.' She rubbed her hands and made for the lodge door. 'And he's absolutely right!'

The next morning, Edwin and Perpetua were woken by a succession of thumps and bumps as Rownan carried bags down from the room upstairs. They offered to help, but Rownan seemed anxious to do it himself.

'Are *you* prepared for today?' he asked them when he'd finished.

'Just about,' Edwin replied, stretching. 'I'm really looking forward to using those instruments on a long journey.'

'And where did you decide to go?'

'Meticulla,' Perpetua butted in. 'Bellwin is taking us to see his uncle and aunt.'

Rownan nodded. 'I am glad that Bellwin is going with you – I would have suggested it myself.' He leant over a bag and dug around inside, rearranging some of the contents. Edwin craned his neck and caught a glimpse of *Ancient Charms of These Territories.*

'Where are you two going?' he asked.

Rownan was silent for a moment as he tied up the top of his bag. 'We have interests . . .' he murmured.

'I am ready, Father.' They heard the voice from above.

At that, Rownan stood up and opened the lodge door. Mornan came down the stairs, walked straight out and strode half a dozen paces into the clearing. Edwin had stopped trying to get a proper look at him – maybe he just had an attack of killer spots. Rownan gathered up the bags.

'We will see you in two days,' he said. 'The navigational tools and maps you need are on the table, and supplies are in the grey bags.'

'Thanks,' Edwin replied. 'Bellwin's bringing some stuff too.'

Rownan nodded and closed the door behind him. Perpetua scurried to the window.

'They had that book!' she trilled. 'Did you see? Where are they going? What are they *doing*?'

'Give it a rest,' Edwin sighed.

Perpetua stomped off to have a wash, and Edwin prepared breakfast. They'd just finished eating when Bellwin arrived. He'd barely tethered the horses and stepped inside before Perpetua told him that Rownan and Mornan had taken *Ancient Charms of These*

Territories on their trip. 'And I asked Rownan what they were up to,' she added indignantly. 'And all he said was that they "had interests".'

'That is what I told you!' Bellwin replied, seemingly surprised by Perpetua's outrage. 'The study of ancient charms makes a fine hobby – nothing more. Now, let us go off to visit my Meticullan relatives.'

Perpetua hauled the rucksack onto her back. 'Imagine if Hildeguard Brolin really *was* your uncle.' She laughed. 'That would be a disaster!'

CHAPTER SIX

'Right – over the next hill, and we're there!'

Edwin folded away the map and dug gently with his heels. His horse began a steady climb. 'We've taken less than five hours – that's pretty good going.'

'Fabulous,' Perpetua groaned. 'My backside is practically numb! Are you sure this was my idea? Why didn't one of you tell me how long it was going to take?'

'But Perpetua, I *did*,' Bellwin said carefully, 'when you asked me.'

Edwin shook his head. 'That's you all over, Perpetua. You get a bee in your bonnet – stuff goes in one ear and straight out the other – then we all get it in the neck.'

Perpetua gave Edwin a hard stare, then turned to

Bellwin. 'He means I get an idea that I won't drop. And I'm so excited that I don't listen. Then everyone else has to suffer the consequences.'

Bellwin raised his eyebrows, but he didn't say anything.

'Now listen, Edwin,' Perpetua said, moving on. 'We haven't talked about *you* – do we tell Brolin that you're Auvlin, like the last time we were here?'

Edwin looked down at his green velvet tunic and the sword hanging from his leather belt. 'Isn't that a bit of a no-brainer?'

Perpetua sighed heavily.

'He means that's a question that has an obvious answer, Bellwin.' She looked at Edwin. 'Well of course it is!' she hissed. 'Telling Brolin you're not Auvlin, when you look exactly like him, would only lead to confusion and awkward questions.' She flicked a strand of hair over her shoulder. 'We just hadn't said it out loud! It's best to get these things firmly said and out in the open.'

'All right!' Edwin snapped back. 'Don't –'

'And watch what you say,' Perpetua added. 'No-brainer indeed! Just mind your Ps and Qs and concentrate on speaking properly. You did it when we met Brolin before, and you were actually quite convincing.'

Edwin rolled his eyes. 'Mind how you go,' he moaned. 'You almost paid me a compliment . . .'

Edwin steered his horse over the hill and down into the scrubby crevice that was the Spartandine Valley. It was raining, and its muddy creek had turned into a torrent of dirty brown water.

'I hope he's around, after all this,' Edwin called back to the others.

He needn't have worried. They found a tunnel entrance, tied up their horses and scurried along the passage leading to Brolin's door. Hanging on it was the same lopsided sign they remembered from their previous visit.

'*The wizard is in,*' Edwin read. 'Wicked!'

Perpetua glanced at Bellwin as if they were looking after a three year old. 'Edwin!' she barked. 'Ps and Qs!'

'S-o-r-r-y . . . Queen's English from now on. Oops, make that the king's!' Edwin grinned. 'I wonder if Brolin's still shoving that snail inside his ear to sort out his deafness?' He couldn't wait to see the eccentric wizard again.

The door opened and swung back by itself. Everyone peered into the room. Wizard Brolin was sitting at his desk with his mane of rats' tails thrown back and his feet soaking in a bowl of water. His long robe was hitched up over his knobbly knees; his eyes were closed and his mouth was slightly open, as if he'd just dozed off.

'He's sound asleep!' Perpetua said fondly.

'Yesterday was a feasting holiday in Meticulla,' Bellwin whispered. 'He may have had to cure *many* cases of rampant indigestion today.'

Brolin snorted and shuffled in his seat, but his eyes didn't open. 'Another case of wind . . .' he muttered, '. . . how extraordinarily blustery it is today.' He sighed and scratched his nose. 'Take your light breeze with you, sir. I am a very busy man . . .'

Edwin had to bite his lip to stop himself laughing. Bellwin took a few steps, leaned forward and touched Brolin's hand. Brolin's eyes opened wide; he shot to his feet, fumbled for his glasses and put them on.

'Bellwin!' Brolin smiled broadly as he identified the young wizard. 'My dear friend!' He stepped out of the bowl. '*And* Prince Auvlin . . .' He bowed. 'I have been hoping my charms are working for you. Oh, and the *delightful* young woman . . .' Brolin screwed up his eyes, and he tapped at his forehead as if he was playing the piano. Finally he punched the air with both fists. 'Yes, I have it! Lady Perpetua – from the Eastern Lands!'

Perpetua beamed and stepped into the room. 'You remember me!'

Brolin took her hand. 'How could I forget? You make *quite* an impression.'

'You can say that again,' Edwin huffed.

'Why thank you, Your Royal Highness,' Brolin replied. He turned back to Perpetua. 'You make quite an impression, my lady.'

Edwin and Perpetua tried to stay serious and sat down with Brolin and Bellwin at a large table. Perpetua tried to peer at Brolin's left ear through a mass of tangled hair. 'Have you, er, got a snail in already?' she said queasily. 'Can you hear us properly – you don't need to lip-read?'

Brolin grinned. 'Oh, no – this snail remedy has proved particularly reliable.' He brushed his rats' tails to one side. 'If you look closely, you should be able to see the little fellow snuggled inside the auditory canal.'

Perpetua swallowed and leant forward.

'Poke him with your finger. Go on! Go on!' he urged as Perpetua shrank back. 'You will do him no harm!'

'I'll do it!' Edwin cried, and he lunged forward. He felt something slimy run across his fingertip. 'That's gross!'

Perpetua shot Edwin a dirty look. 'He said "that's close"!' she added pointedly.

Bellwin looked at them, sighed and shook his head.

'Brolin,' he said. 'How are you?

'Exhausted!' Brolin replied. 'Yesterday was a feasting day . . . Meticullans are well known for their love of food – and *who* is it who relieves them from the symptoms of over-indulgence?' He leaned in, and mouthed, 'I have not seen so much wind since greenacre sprouts were served at the wedding of my great-nephew.'

'I thought as much,' Bellwin said. 'Is the worst over?'

'Yes, my friend – the complaint rushes in like a hurricane, gives twelve hours of agony then blows itself out.' Brolin blinked. 'Literally.'

'So are you too tired to see us?' Bellwin asked gently. 'We wished to talk with you at length.'

The elderly wizard smiled. 'I have taken a nap . . . and the sight of dear friends *always* rouses the senses!' He looked at Edwin. 'Is it the spell I cast on you, Auvlin? Have you returned for more treatment?'

Edwin gave a nervous cough, trying to remember exactly what Bellwin had told him. 'No, what you told Bellwin before was right – the spell *has* started working again, and I'm almost recovered. In fact, I was the one who led us here, without so much as a wrong turning! We just wanted to talk to you about something.'

'What is it you wish to discuss?'

Perpetua crossed her arms and said, 'Shadow Magic.'

Brolin looked hard at Bellwin. 'Your interest has been aroused by our *last* conversation.' He frowned. 'I must be sure you do not mean to *practise* the art . . .'

'Oh, no!' Bellwin assured him. 'Nothing is further from my mind. We mean to find out more about Shadow Magic so that Hysteria may be better guarded against the Umbrians.'

Brolin pushed his glasses up his nose. 'Then I will be very happy to help!' He sprang to his feet. 'Can I offer you something to eat? Many of my patients brought me food from the feasting, and I shall *never* eat it all on my own . . .'

Edwin and Perpetua had never had a seven course tea before, and Bellwin kept going far longer than they did. He ate while Brolin talked to him about Shadow Magic, and once Bellwin had finished his second piece of junoberry cream pie he pulled a quill and a piece of parchment from his bag.

'Now,' he said, 'I must write that last part down.'

'Very wise,' Brolin remarked. 'The method the Umbrians use to prepare their crystals is especially important.'

'The Umbrians don't have many crystals, do they?' Edwin asked.

'No – they have only two mines, both of which contain a very mixed quality of crystals. Whereas, as I am sure you are aware, Hysteria has more than twenty mines, and most of the crystals they yield are of a superior quality.'

Edwin nodded. 'So do the Umbrians tend to *save* their crystals for spells like transformation?'

'It is thought so. Spells such as those require an enormous amount of magical power, so the Umbrians are unlikely to waste any on petty charms.' Brolin looked at Bellwin. 'Hysterian wizards should count themselves fortunate!'

'I specialise in petty charms!' Bellwin boasted. Then he put on a serious face. 'Can you tell us about transformation, Brolin – how is it done?'

'It is a complicated spell, and one that takes many

weeks to complete. To transform a person into the image of another, a piece of tissue is needed from the man or woman they will look like. It could be a shred of fingernail or a single hair – but from that the spell takes all the information needed to complete the transformation.'

'DNA,' Perpetua whispered, her jaw dropping. 'He's talking about DNA!'

Edwin's eyes widened. Even *he* had heard of that.

'So the tissue gives everything?' Bellwin said. 'The colour of the eyes, the thickness of the hair – and the magic transfers it *all* onto the subject of the spell?'

'No, not quite,' Brolin replied. 'The subject always retains one feature of themselves so that, if required, they may be transformed back into their original form. This feature, for reasons that even the Umbrians do not understand, is dictated by the tissue taken from the other person. For example,' he added, looking at Perpetua. 'If ten people were transformed into the image of *you*, my lady, they would retain the same one feature – your eye colour, perhaps.'

'But *that* would be no use at all,' Perpetua said. 'The difference between me and them would be obvious!'

'That is only an example – there are many features that are hidden and the difference would not be noticed.'

'Of course,' Bellwin said, scribbling in a notebook. 'Who notices the shape of anyone else's toe nails or the size of their nostrils?'

Edwin bent down and squinted upwards at Perpetua. 'Now you mention it . . .'

'*And,*' Brolin continued, 'the person who has been transformed keeps their own soul . . . their own consciousness. They may have received a copy of the brain matter and sensory ability of the other person, but their knowledge, thoughts, feelings and ambitions are still entirely their own.'

'Yes!' Perpetua scoffed. 'So they can do horrible things to nice people!' She looked at Brolin. 'Have *you* seen transformation being done?'

'No, but a friend of mine has . . . very recently. And her account of it was most disturbing.'

Edwin held his breath. 'How do you mean?'

Brolin took a large gulp of red wine. 'Agnetha takes an interest in all kinds of magic, and only a week ago she took a disguise to gain access to what is the heart of the Umbrian circle of wizards.'

Brolin looked at Bellwin, who said, 'So this has happened since the last time we met. Where was this – the Umbrian fort?'

'No, my friend. Apparently there is a large villa – further into Umbrian territory – where the wizards gather to practise and to teach their apprentices. It was in a room under the house – deep underground – that Agnetha witnessed the culmination of the transformation process. A boy was transformed into another boy although who the boys were she did not know. But then Agnetha would recognise very few people as she rarely ventures into the outside world.'

Edwin and Perpetua looked at each other. This was serious stuff.

'So . . . what else did she see?' Perpetua asked.

'Let me think. I recorded some of the conversations Agnetha and I had.' Brolin turned to a shelf and leafed through a number of notebooks. 'Here it is! Now . . . the Umbrian wizard held a small vessel, and inside it was the human tissue from which the transformation took place – although Agnetha was not close enough to see what the tissue was.' Brolin paused for a moment. 'She told me the spell had been conjured weeks before, and in that time the magic had read all the information contained in the tissue. Well, a thick smoke rose from the jar and streamed into the mouth of the boy. He began to choke almost at once. Poor child . . . his body convulsed, he became covered in sweat. Agnetha and the other observers left the room for a few hours, and in that time the boy's body and face changed completely. Except, of course, for the one feature that was retained.'

'Did Agnetha notice what the feature was?' Bellwin asked.

'No. It was impossible to tell.' Brolin sighed. 'There was worse to come. Once the transformation was complete, the Umbrians subjected the boy to a brutal examination. They took a magical instrument that had a very powerful light, and shone it straight into his eyes. Agnetha told me she could not sleep for days afterwards – she could still hear the boy's screams when she lay down at night.'

Edwin swallowed. 'That's horrible. What were they *doing* to him?'

'It was not clear, Auvlin – Agnetha thought the Umbrians were trying to look inside the boy's eyes, that they were searching for something.' Brolin fixed on Edwin with an uncharacteristically steely gaze. 'Although she did say this – once the examination had finished, the barbarian who had held the instrument demanded more work on what he called *full replication*.'

Edwin and Perpetua looked at Bellwin, but he just shrugged. 'Full replication' obviously meant nothing to him. Perpetua busily reviewed her notes while Edwin tried to look as if he'd retained as much information as she had.

'My friends, it is very late,' Brolin said after a few moments. He stretched his back. 'It is wonderful to talk with you, but I am afraid I must rest. Are you staying here tonight, in Wizard Brolin's humble underground cavern?'

Bellwin nodded. 'We had hoped to – we have sleeping bags and everything we need to wash.'

Brolin got to his feet, reached for a piece of rag and tied his straggly hair at the very top of his head. He looked like a mangy pineapple. 'There – my bedtime preparations are complete. I shall leave you lively young people to talk amongst yourselves.' He scurried off to his room. 'Goodnight!'

Edwin, Perpetua and Bellwin got ready for bed, then arranged their sleeping bags on the floor. They all started yawning; suddenly, it seemed the journey from Hysteria had caught up with them.

'You know,' Perpetua yawned before she fell asleep. 'Eifus may be right – I don't think Brolin *does* wash his hair.'

CHAPTER SEVEN

The next morning, they were woken by the sound of scuffling and thumping from the other side of the front door. Brolin emerged from his room with a scowl, opened the door and peered outside.

'Wizard Brolin,' said an anxious voice, 'my ailment has returned. The discomfort is most discomforting!'

Brolin tut-tutted and pointed to his sign. 'What pray, does *this* say? *The wizard is asleep.*' Then he sighed. 'Very well . . . what did you eat for supper last night?'

There was a long pause, before the patient mumbled, 'Turnip mash.'

'Turnip mash?' Brolin cried. 'I did not prescribe

that! I said Peppermint milk and hot oils and that nothing else would do!'

'But my wife *made* the mash,' the man said meekly. 'It was so good, I could not resist . . .'

'Then, alas,' Brolin said grandly, 'I offer no further assistance. I cannot help those who will not help themselves.' He swivelled on his heel and slammed the door. There was a muffled, 'Ouch!'

Brolin looked at his guests, who were now wide awake. 'Good morning! Excuse me while I exercise!' Brolin stretched, then shook his head violently. The old rag in his hair – which had almost worked its way out – shot across the room and his rat's tales fanned out like peacock feathers.

'Exercise complete!' Brolin said briskly. He clutched his stomach. 'Now it is time for breakfast. I know it is unusual at this hour – but shall we try some vanilla and hazelnut cake?'

Perpetua didn't approve, and chose seaweed bread and dried fish. But Bellwin and Edwin tucked in, each eating three slices of cake before they said another word. Once Edwin had finished, he noticed that Perpetua had turned slightly green.

'Er, Brolin,' she said, pushing her plate away. 'Auvlin and I meant to ask you – how does practising Shadow Magic turn a person into someone that drinks blood?'

Brolin picked up a napkin and dabbed his mouth, as if he was trying to collect his thoughts. 'It is all to do with the blood,' he replied. 'As I am sure you know, these territories are ruled by Ancient Magical Lore – when the Lore was laid down, it was deemed any person breaking it should pay a price.'

'What price?' Perpetua asked.

'Their blood slowly loses its vital elements, resulting in death.' Brolin calmly took his fourth piece of cake. 'The Umbrians, of course, break Ancient Magical Lore every time they practise Shadow Magic. But hundreds of years ago they found a way to evade the curse – quite simply, they drink the blood of other humans. This gives them *back* the vitality their blood needs.'

Edwin stopped eating and swallowed hard. 'Blimey – er – goodness. How much do they have to drink, and how often?'

'As the loss of vitality is slow they need only take a little blood, once a week.'

'What? A handful . . . a cupful?'

Brolin held up an unfinished glass of red liquid. 'About this much,' he replied. He looked around the table. 'Oh . . . would you care for raspberry wine with your breakfast?'

Everyone shook their head.

'Where do the Umbrians *get* the blood?' Bellwin asked.

'I do not know,' Brolin murmured. 'And it is a question that has troubled me for a very long time.' He roused himself. 'To return to our discussion – the consumption of another creature's blood has an effect on the entire chemistry of the body. For example, the person is not comfortable in bright light . . . there are certain foods they cannot tolerate . . . and, rather worryingly, they do not die in the way that *other humans* do.'

Edwin caught Perpetua's eye and whispered, 'Too right!'

She frowned back and mouthed, 'Ps and Qs!'

'It is fascinating,' Bellwin said quietly. 'Do you mind if we stay with you until mid-morning? There is so much more I would like to learn.'

Brolin smiled. 'My friend, you may stay as long as you wish. What else would you like to know?'

A few hours later, Edwin and Perpetua scrambled up into their saddles and watched the two wizards shake hands. Bellwin had wanted to find out about everything Agnetha had seen at the Umbrian villa, and Brolin had decided to give him notes he'd made of his conversations with her.

'Thank you, Brolin,' said Bellwin. 'I only hope I can put your knowledge to good use one day.'

'It is a pleasure to teach such a fine young wizard. Perhaps, like me, you will eventually take up work in ailments and worries – you would have an exceptional bedside manner!'

Bellwin blushed and turned to mount his horse.

'Do you have enough supplies for the journey?' Brolin called. 'Lady Perpetua – my dried fish and seaweed bread are entirely at your disposal.'

Perpetua forced a smile. 'Thank you, but I really couldn't eat another thing!'

Brolin beamed. 'Then it is time for us to part. But first – more excercise.' He did one star jump, then took a deep breath. 'Ah, that is better. I do hope you have a safe journey home. Goodbye, my friends. Goodbye!'

It was very late in the afternoon and the journey back from Meticulla was nearly at an end. There had been lots of conversation to pass the time – Bellwin proudly described the exquisite banquet Janus had held in his honour; Edwin tried to explain football and the offside rule; Perpetua gave a detailed account of how she'd become Templeton Grove Comp's top performer in Science.

'You wanna get a life,' Edwin had grunted. Perpetua didn't bother to translate.

The horses plodded towards a line of trees that Edwin knew wasn't far from the lodge.

'We shall arrive just before the sun goes down,' Bellwin said. 'It was good to see Wizard Brolin again – what interesting things he had to tell us.'

'Oh, yes,' Perpetua replied. 'If a bit gruesome!'

'I don't like the sound of what that woman saw,' Edwin said grimly. 'All that horrible stuff with the boy. Bellwin, d'you think the Umbrians are up to something?'

'I do not know,' Bellwin replied. 'Ollwin has told me the Umbrians have always experimented – why, thousands of years ago they pushed the boundaries of white magic to *create* Shadow Magic.'

'But all experiments have a purpose,' Perpetua announced. 'And the one Agnetha witnessed will be no different.'

'Well, I suppose we have to hope it has no bearing on *us*,' Bellwin sighed.

The dusk gathered as they progressed deeper into the forest; they were quiet now that their journey was near its end. The way through the trees became hard to follow, and Edwin's horse, Spur, led the others from the path and down into a hollow. Spur picked his way amongst the deep bracken, Edwin swaying in his saddle. Suddenly, his mount reared. Edwin clung on as he veered crazily to the left. Spur's hooves stamped the ground then he trotted forward, snorting with fright. Edwin pulled the rein and smoothed the stallion's neck.

'What is it, boy?' he whispered. 'What is it?'

Bellwin dismounted and ran over. 'Something scared him!' He grabbed the rein and Edwin jumped to the ground.

'Did you see?'

'Over there.'

Edwin walked forward, his eyes scouring the tangle of fern and bracken. Suddenly, there was movement. Perpetua squealed. Edwin stopped in his tracks.

A few metres ahead, a hand rose up from the sea of vegetation. It was pale and bony. The hand trembled, as if the effort was too much, then the fingers curled and it fell back.

Edwin took a shaky breath. He looked at Bellwin, then to Perpetua. They stared back; silent, hesitant. Edwin put a finger to his lips then took another step. He craned his neck, almost too scared to look. There was a gap in the bracken. He edged forward to see clothes, legs . . . an arm. It was . . .

'A boy,' Edwin murmured.

Bellwin helped Perpetua to the ground and they scrambled over to where Edwin was crouched. Bellwin signalled them both to stay where they were and knelt down, cradling the boy's head in his hands. The boy's eyes were closed; his mouth was slurred with pain. His face was pale and thin, but it was one they all recognised.

'Auvlin?' Perpetua whispered.

Edwin shook his head. 'No, but someone who we thought looked like him.'

Perpetua stared at her friend. 'Before . . . here in the forest?'

'He's wearing the same tunic. He's got marks around

his wrists as if he's been chained.' Edwin looked at Bellwin. 'This is the boy we told you about. He was riding with a man and woman.'

Bellwin swallowed. 'By Janus, he looks *exactly* like Prince Auvlin.' He shook his head. 'This means –'

The boy let out a gurgled moan. He tried to raise himself, but collapsed back into Bellwin's arms.

'Please . . . help me,' he whispered.

Perpetua knelt down and took the boy's hand. 'We're not going to hurt you,' she said, but her voice was trembling. 'Don't worry – you're going to be all right.'

The boy's eyelids fluttered again, and he grasped Perpetua's fingers.

'Can you look at me?' she asked gently.

The boy held his breath. He whimpered; it seemed he couldn't do as Perpetua had asked.

'What have they done to you?' Bellwin began to cry. Tears splashed onto the boy's face and ran down the hollow of his cheek. Almost imperceptibly, the boy squeezed Perpetua's hand.

'I'm here,' she said, trying to keep her voice calm. 'We'll look after you.'

But at that moment, the boy's head slumped to one side. He took a shallow breath; there was a long gap, then another tiny breath. His grip on Perpetua loosened, he let out a strange, low sigh and his mouth fell slack. There was no more movement; no more gasps for air. Just a long, heavy silence.

'He's dead,' Edwin whispered, dropping to his knees. 'They've killed him . . . the Umbrians have killed him.'

Perpetua looked at Edwin, but she didn't question what he'd said. Instead she stroked the boy's hand one last time, and placed it by his side. Bellwin wiped his tears from the boy's cheek, then gently lay his lifeless head on the bed of bracken.

'Edwin,' Bellwin said in a low voice. 'The man and woman you saw – did you recognise them?'

'No, we didn't,' Edwin replied weakly.

'The boy seemed to be their prisoner,' Perpetua croaked. 'His hands were tied and he was wearing a metal mask. We only caught a glimpse of his face when he needed a drink and the woman took the mask off.' She swallowed a gulp. 'Poor thing . . .'

Bellwin took a deep breath. 'I do not know what the Umbrians are planning – but this . . .' He pointed to the body. '*This* means danger.'

Perpetua struggled to her feet. 'Then we should get back . . .'

'But what about the boy?' Edwin said.

Bellwin grabbed both their hands and pulled them towards the horses. 'An hour or two ago we might have saved him – but he is beyond that now. We need to save *ourselves*.'

Perpetua's chin began to shake; she looked quickly around the forest. 'D'you think those people are going to come back for the body?'

'I do not know,' Bellwin replied.

They quickly mounted their horses and steered them out of the hollow.

'He might not have a proper burial,' Edwin murmured, gazing back.

Bellwin's horse led the way this time, trotting briskly through the gaps in the trees. Edwin ducked between the branches, peering into every dim shaft of light. Every shape and shadow caught his eye, his stomach aching with more and more tension as each second passed.

'The lodge is just the other side of this clearing,' Edwin said quietly after a while. 'It's only a few minutes away.'

'Thank God,' Perpetua whined. 'I don't think I've ever been –'

CRACK!

Just as they cleared the trees, there was the sound of splintering wood from behind. Edwin looked back. A huge black horse exploded through the trees towards them, leaving a branch skewed to one side. A cloak covered the rider's face as he bent low over the animal's neck, urging it on, cracking a whip against his mount's inky coat. Suddenly a second horse jumped the thicket and began to race after him.

'RIDE!' Edwin yelled. He dug his heels, forcing Spur to gallop towards the other side of the clearing. He glanced back. Bellwin and Perpetua were neck and neck, their horses' hooves flicking soil with each dull thud. Edwin took a gulp of air and blinked against the rush of cold air. He looked back again. The black horse was catching them, nostrils flaring, eyes wide and wild.

'COME ON!' Edwin screamed. 'THEY'RE GONNA GET US!'

He dug his heels again, pushing his hands onto his horse's mane urging him faster and faster. They flew back into the forest. Edwin steered between two trees and jumped over a thicket. He heard Perpetua shriek and glanced back. She'd made it, but was hanging on for dear life.

'Keep going!' Bellwin's voice rose above the thundering hooves. 'We are losing them!'

Gasps shuddered in and out of Edwin's chest as the lodge came into sight. He skirted a tree stump, pulled the rein and jumped to the ground, leaving his horse to wander towards the grass.

'Quickly!' he yelled. Bellwin and Perpetua weren't far behind. But their pursuers were still in sight.

'It's no use,' Perpetua squealed as Edwin pulled her down from the saddle. 'They must *know* we're coming here . . .'

Bellwin shoved the door open and bundled Edwin and Perpetua through, closing the door behind them. There was no sign of Rownan.

'Hide!' Edwin said, looking around frantically.

'There!' Perpetua pointed upwards.

They rattled up the stairs and looked around. 'There is nowhere *to* hide,' Bellwin muttered.

'The cupboards!' Edwin opened a door and pulled bundles of clothes to the floor.

'That's the first place they'll look!' Perpetua whined. 'What are –'

From below, the front door creaked.

Edwin felt his heart thump in his throat. He took Bellwin and Perpetua's hands and led them past the pale light from the bedroom window and into the shadows. They stood, all three, with their backs against the wall, rigid with fear.

Footsteps downstairs. An inner door opened . . . the sound of muffled whispers. Then a footstep on the stairs. Another, then a third. Edwin looked around desperately for something to fight with, but there was nothing. He tried to shrink backwards, edging his feet against the wall.

Another footstep. Edwin heard Perpetua swallow. A dark hooded figure rose slowly onto the first floor. It glanced the other way, then turned. It was looking straight at them. The shape of another figure climbed the stairs, turned and pointed a gloved hand towards them.

Edwin tried to whisper, 'Go away . . .' but instead he swallowed against a lifeless tongue. The two faceless figures advanced, step by slow step. They passed into the pale light of the dusk, and stopped. The first raised a hand to his hood. The sword hanging from his waist shone a soft glint.

'Edwin . . .' Perpetua cried, 'do something!'

He clenched his fists as the hood was torn back . . .

'Edwin Spencer!' Janus cried. 'What in the name of Hysteria are you doing here?'

CHAPTER EIGHT

Edwin collapsed into Janus's arms. He'd never experienced such a tidal wave of relief. As soon as he felt the king's warm hug, all thoughts of Auvlin's secret plan faded.

'Does he seem to be hurt?' Edwin heard a familiar voice say. It was Primus.

'Father,' Edwin croaked. 'I mean Janus . . . I mean Your Majesty . . .'

Janus gripped Edwin's shoulders and stared at him, his eyes shining. 'Do not worry, my boy,' he whispered. 'How glad I am to see you.' He smiled, then frowned and shook his head. 'But I must ask you again – why *are* you here?'

It took quite a while to explain why Edwin and Perpetua were back in Hysteria. Once Perpetua got her breath back she almost took over and Edwin had to butt in every time she got too carried away. Janus sat in silence through the whole thing; Primus kept raising his hands in apparent disbelief.

'What was Auvlin thinking?' he cried. 'Letting you travel around the forest with only a novice wizard for protection!'

Edwin and Bellwin glanced at each other and winced. Janus and Primus were angry . . . seriously angry, and they hadn't yet been told about Wizard Brolin or the body in the forest.

'You don't know the half of it,' Edwin murmured.

'He means that's not the whole story,' Perpetua said primly. 'We've been *much* further than that, *and* –'

Janus frowned. 'Where?' he said simply.

Belwin shuffled in his seat. 'To Meticulla to . . . to see Wizard Brolin.'

Janus sprang to his feet. 'What?' He hesitated, then looked at the ceiling and took a deep breath. 'We will hear the rest of what you have to say at the castle – Ollwin will be especially interested in the conclusion of your story.' He looked back at Bellwin, then to Edwin and Perpetua. 'Your collusion with my son has come to an end.'

Bellwin couldn't raise his gaze, but the children got to their feet.

'Your Majesty,' Perpetua said carefully. 'How did you know we were here?'

'We did *not* know,' Janus replied. 'But there have been sightings of unknown riders in the forest . . . and some curious incidents at the crystal mines. Primus and I decided to ride out at dusk to look for ourselves.'

'We saw you from a distance,' Primus added. 'You looked nervous . . . so we gave chase.'

'So no one gave the plan away?' Edwin asked. 'Eifus and Dreifus, or Rownan?'

Janus shook his head. 'No.'

'But . . . but they won't get in trouble?'

Janus swung his cloak over his shoulders. He stared at Edwin, then broke a half-smile.

'No, Edwin,' he said softly. 'They were carrying out the requests of my son, and for that I cannot blame them.' He put his hand on Edwin's shoulder. 'You have not changed – you are always concerned for the welfare of others. But it is Auvlin who must carry the blame for all this. And as soon as we arrive back at the castle, we shall also hear *his* side of the story.'

Edwin and Perpetua quickly packed their things and left a note for Rownan trying to explain what had happened.

As they trotted through the forest, Bellwin didn't say a word. Edwin knew why – he was *terrified* of what Ollwin would say. But Edwin felt OK. He was buzzing.

He was with Janus again; he was heading back to Emporium Castle. And for Edwin, it didn't get any better than that.

A bit later, Edwin almost skipped along the passage towards the throne room. Perpetua walked briskly behind. She'd settled into her room and got over the fact that there'd be no more exploration of Hysteria's flora and fauna – she was looking forward to a nice soft bed.

They found the king on his throne. He'd changed into his customary robes, and sat back with a hand to his mouth, deep in thought. Auvlin stood beside him.

'Sorry . . .' Edwin mouthed. The only response was a hard stare.

'We will wait for Ollwin and Lorius to arrive,' Janus said. 'Primus has gone to fetch them.'

Edwin grimaced at Perpetua at the mention of their old science teacher. 'I'd forgotten about Lorius.'

She leant towards him. 'He'll turn us to stone with just one glance.'

They waited in silence until footsteps tapped along the adjoining passage. Edwin turned. Primus led the way with his quick, athletic stride, the towering figure of Lorius followed, his black cloak floating in his wake. Last came Ollwin, short and round and rushing to keep up.

Janus sat up. 'My lords,' he said. 'You will see we have some unexpected guests.'

Ollwin came to an abrupt stop. He looked at Auvlin, then the children.

'*Edwin and Perpetua*?' Ollwin said with an incredulous smile. But the smile faded when he noticed Bellwin, and he said, 'What has happened?'

Lorius didn't say anything. He just glared at Edwin.

'I will let Auvlin explain,' Janus said simply.

The Prince took his time to begin. '*I* asked Edwin to come to Hysteria,' he said eventually.

'He didn't ask *me*,' Perpetua pipped up. 'I'm afraid I invited myself!'

Ollwin, who didn't look at all surprised, said to Auvlin, '*Why* did you ask Edwin to come here?'

'I am to compete in the Pan Kingdom triathlon very soon as you know, but I am afraid my sense of direction is *still* not as it used to be. I did not want to tell my father – I did not want to worry him – so I asked Edwin to take my place in the orienteering discipline. He has been staying at the lodge of Rownan the Woodsman – Rownan has been teaching him about the terrain.'

Ollwin frowned. 'Back to the start, Auvlin – *you are not cured*?'

'It seems not . . .'

'But Wizard Brolin gave a guarantee that his treatment would work!'

'Yes,' Janus agreed. 'But that is for later. Much more

importantly, Auvlin has embarked on a plan that is both deceitful and dangerous. He has coerced Bellwin into using an enormous amount of magical power *without* your permission, *and* he has put our friends Edwin and Perpetua in danger.'

'Very well,' Ollwin said. 'But once this issue is dealt with, I will pay Wizard Brolin a visit to investigate this anomaly.'

'Actually, Master,' Bellwin said weakly. 'Prince Auvlin has already sent me back to see him.'

'That . . . that is right,' Auvlin added nervously. 'Tell them what he told you, Bellwin – you do remember what he said? *Tell them.*'

'Of course.' Bellwin turned back to Ollwin. 'Brolin was very surprised the spell had not worked. He mentioned his guarantee, so I am sure he has not tried to deceive us in any way. But he *also* said spells such as the one he performed on Auvlin can diminish, then lay dormant for some time before they start to work again – it happens rarely, but it *can* occur.' Bellwin shook his head. 'It was the only explanation he could offer, but he is sure his spell will gain strength very soon.'

'So that is why my sense of direction is still impaired, Ollwin,' Auvlin said quickly. 'There is no other reason. None at all.'

Ollwin hesitated, then gave a nod. 'I have heard of this phenomenon. Perhaps I have been too quick to judge – we will take Brolin's advice, and give the treatment more time.' But he wasn't finished. He narrowed his eyes at Bellwin. 'So *you* brought Edwin and Perpetua here? And aged him, too?'

Bellwin nodded. He knew what was coming.

'What in the name of Janus were YOU DOING?' Ollwin bellowed. 'I expected no more nonsense once you achieved Full Wizarding! How do you –'

'Ollwin!' Janus said impatiently. 'Leave the boy! What do you expect a novice wizard to do when pressured by the heir to the throne? Bellwin is young enough that one day Auvlin will be *his* monarch. No one but my son is to blame for this regrettable situation.'

Ollwin sighed heavily. 'If you wish, Your Majesty.' He looked at Bellwin. 'You are forgiven,' he added grudgingly.

'Thank you, master,' Bellwin mumbled. 'But I have *something else* to tell you . . .'

Ollwin almost growled.

Perpetua stepped forward. 'Let *me* tell them – it was my idea,' she said firmly. 'Ollwin – Bellwin told us you were worried about the Umbrians. He said he'd been to see Brolin about Auvlin's treatment, and mentioned that Hildeguard Brolin knew an awful lot about Shadow Magic. *I* suggested that Bellwin could learn from Brolin – it seems to *me* the more you know about Shadow Magic, the easier it'd be to defeat the Umbrians.'

'Rownan and his son had to go away for a few days,' Edwin continued. 'He said while they were away I could practise orienteering with Hysterian tools. Perpetua and I persuaded Bellwin we should go to Meticulla.'

'We stayed with Brolin for one night,' Perpetua added. 'And we learnt *loads* about Shadow Magic.'

Ollwin stared at Bellwin disapprovingly, but Bellwin took a deep breath. 'Wizard Brolin has a wealth of knowledge . . .' He scrabbled in his bag for some notes. 'I found out how the Umbrians prepare their crystals . . . how they train their apprentices . . . and . . . and a little about how transformation works.'

Ollwin continued to look at Bellwin, then shook his head. 'You are treading on dangerous territory,' he said gravely. 'This information will be useful, no doubt – but I fear even a little knowledge of Shadow Magic can draw in *anyone*.'

'But of that there is no danger,' Bellwin replied. 'As I have already said, Brolin's knowledge is *vast*, and he is no more tainted by Shadow Magic than you or I.'

'He's right!' Perpetua trilled. 'Brolin may be very eccentric, but he's obviously a very honest man.'

Ollwin hesitated, then reached out for the notes. 'You may well be right, Perpetua, but to meddle in Shadow Magic requires very serious thought.' He flicked through a few pages. 'Bellwin, come to my workshop later – we will look at these together.'

'Yes, master,' Bellwin said with relief. But then he seemed to steel himself again. 'We must also tell you – on our way back to the lodge tonight, we made a terrible discovery in the forest.'

Once again Perpetua took over, of which Bellwin looked quite glad. She repeated everything that she and Edwin had seen in the forest – the riders, the boy, and how he had seemed to be held by force.

'Actually we thought . . . we thought he looked a bit like Auvlin,' Perpetua concluded nervously.

Edwin swallowed. 'Tonight we found the boy lying on the forest floor. And . . . and he looked *exactly* like Auvlin.'

Janus shot to his feet, his face aghast. 'Like my son?' He looked desperately from Ollwin to Primus. 'This can be no coincidence! The Umbrians are using transformation . . . they are planning our destruction – again!' He strode to Auvlin and gripped his shoulders. 'They shall not have my boy!' He wrenched Auvlin into his arms. 'You are safe with us . . . they will not take you from me again.'

Auvlin stood very still, as if he were just waiting to be released. 'I know, Father . . .' he mumbled. As soon as Janus let go, he backed away.

Janus quickly descended the steps from his throne. 'Where is this boy?' he demanded.

Edwin glanced at the others. 'He . . . he died.'

The king's face drained white, and for a moment he

101

was unable to speak. 'How did the boy die?' he asked eventually.

'We don't know. We didn't dare bring back his body. We wanted to get away in case the man and the woman were still around . . .'

Janus swallowed, then turned to Bellwin. 'What else did you find out from Brolin? What did you learn about transformation?'

'I know where it takes place,' Bellwin replied. 'Not within the Umbrian fort, but in a villa deeper into their territory. A few weeks ago, a friend of Brolin's saw a boy being transformed into the image of *another* boy.' He hesitated. 'It could have been the one Edwin found in the forest,' he said quickly. 'Or perhaps *another* boy made to look like Auvlin . . .'

'I fear you may be right,' Janus said gravely. He shut his eyes for a moment. 'Bellwin, I want to hear *everything* Brolin told you. And in the morning we will all gather to make our plans.'

Auvlin took a step forward. 'Plans, Father?' he said, sounding puzzled.

'Yes!' Janus said almost impatiently. 'What would you have me do – wait until the Umbrians have ten of you, and are beating down our door to replace you with one of their own?'

'No,' Auvlin replied; suddenly looking more anxious than ever. 'But . . . but I am worried for our safety. For *your* safety, Father.'

'Auvlin, the king is right,' Primus said. 'We must act now. And look around you – every one of us who faced the Umbrian threat before stands here, alive and well.'

'That includes you, Auvlin!' Perpetua said excitedly. 'And you were practically dead!'

Janus climbed back up to his throne. 'Primus, send some men to fetch this boy's body – Edwin will tell you where to find it. Bellwin, I want to know everything that has happened since Edwin and Perpetua arrived here. Auvlin, once Bellwin has finished, you and I will speak in private.'

Auvlin looked at the floor. 'Yes, Father . . .'

CHAPTER NINE

Poor Bellwin. As he gave his faltering account of the past few days, Ollwin's gaze followed him like a fox staring through chicken wire. It was only when the topic of Shadow Magic came up that Ollwin looked down at the notes.

'You forgot to write that part down!' he hissed, scribbling furiously.

'Then we must praise the boy's memory!' Janus cut in. 'He is doing his best.'

Edwin and Perpetua were asked lots of questions by Janus and Primus; but Lorius sat quietly throughout the whole thing, only looking up once or twice to cast a cold stare. It was almost like old times at Templeton

Grove Comp. When they'd finished, Janus bid them all goodnight and left with Auvlin. Ollwin ushered a chastened-looking Bellwin out of the room along with the others.

'I'm surprised he didn't drag him away by his ear!' Perpetua whispered as she and Edwin followed a servant along a passage.

'Yeah,' Edwin agreed. 'Ollwin was *well* mad.'

The servant left them in Edwin's room. It wasn't a patch on where he'd stayed the last time. The bed was quite small, and the blankets were only woollen, not soft and silky like those he'd had in the royal suite.

'I've come down in the world,' Edwin sighed. 'In this one, anyway.'

'Well, Janus has the real heir to his throne now,' Perpetua said matter-of-factly. 'What do you want him to do – throw Auvlin out of his apartments just because *you've* arrived?' She sniffed. 'Anyway, this was the sort of thing *I* had before, and what's good enough for me is good enough for you.'

'Yeah, yeah, yeah . . .' Edwin slouched onto the bed.

Perpetua sat beside him and crossed her arms. 'So, what are we going to do?'

Edwin cast her a sideways glance. 'What do you *want* to do – go home?'

Perpetua thought for a moment, then shook her head. 'No,' she murmured. 'I want to stay . . . I want to stay and help them.'

Edwin stared at her, then broke a half-smile. 'Me too . . . if we can.' He shrugged. 'But what can *we* do?'

'Who knows?' Perpetua said lightly. 'And that's what's so exciting!' She stood up. 'Now I'm going to my room. Don't be too long in getting to sleep.'

'Don't worry,' Edwin replied, yawning. 'I intend to get as much kip as I can . . .'

Edwin got ready for bed in world-record time, and was asleep before his head hit the pillow.

Unfortunately, as kips go this one wasn't the longest. Only a few hours later a hand was placed on Edwin's shoulder; he came to, squinting against candlelight.

'Edwin,' he heard a soft voice whisper. 'Do not be afraid. I am sorry − it is the middle of the night, but I cannot wait.'

'Janus,' Edwin murmured. 'Your Majesty . . . what is it? Have Primus's men found the body?'

The king sat on the bed, shaking his head. 'It had already been taken from the forest. No, Edwin, I want to talk to you.'

Edwin scratched his head and sat up. Janus's smile was warm; his eyes shone with affection. He took Edwin's hand and squeezed it tight. 'My heart is bursting with happiness at the very sight of you. I have *missed you*, my boy.'

Edwin felt a lump in his throat, but he resisted the

urge to throw his arms around Janus's neck. This was the king, after all. 'I missed you, too,' he croaked. 'I *really* did.'

They gazed at each other, until Janus said, 'I have often wondered – after you left us, what happened when you arrived home?'

'It was just the same as before – apart from time being rewound. That was *weird*.'

'You misunderstand – I mean your family,' Janus said. 'Were you able to adjust back into life on Earth? Did your family sense a change in you . . . or did they treat you as before?'

Edwin thought for a moment. After he'd got that A for science things *had* changed. His mother had been a lot pushier and his sisters had become very suspicious. Ollie convinced their father that the mark was a fluke, so Mr Spencer took no more interest in Edwin than before. So, if he took the A *out* of the equation . . .

'No,' Edwin said. 'They were all just the same.'

'Good . . . good.' Janus smiled. 'A young man needs the support of his family, especially his parents. Of course, my son has had to do without his mother, but *I* have tried *twice* as hard.'

Edwin smiled. Did Auvlin know how lucky he was?

'Now – the question I want to ask you,' Janus said. 'It concerns Rownan.'

'Oh . . . he was only doing what Auvlin asked him, Your Majesty, the same as –'

Janus shook his head. 'I do not wish to punish him, Edwin. I merely wonder where he went when he left the lodge with his son. The task Auvlin gave him – to teach you about the local terrain – would be difficult to complete in such a short time, so what took him away *must* have been urgent. I am worried that it may have something to do with the riders in the forest.'

'Nah, I don't think so,' Edwin replied. 'I reckon it's to do with one of his hobbies. Me and Perpetua found a book in the lodge about ancient relics, and we saw it in Rownan's bag just before he left.'

'Ancient relics?' Janus repeated. 'Are you sure?'

'Yeah – positive. We told Bellwin about the book, and *he* said that sort of thing makes a good hobby.'

'But a two-day absence – why would . . . ?' Janus paused, then patted Edwin's hand. 'I am sure you are right,' he said quickly. He got to his feet. 'I must let you get back to sleep. Goodnight, Edwin.'

'But, Your Majesty, what –?'

Janus didn't wait to hear Edwin's question; he made for the door without another word. Edwin waited until the latch clicked shut, then he slipped out of bed and inched the door back open. He glimpsed Janus walk along the passage with one of his guards.

'Go and wake the gatekeeper.' Janus's instruction echoed along the stone walls. 'Ask if he has seen Rownan the Woodsman around the castle, we must be sure . . .' Edwin strained to hear the rest, but Janus's voice faded

away. He pushed the door shut, leant against it and screwed up his nose. What was *that* all about?
'

The next morning, Bellwin brought breakfast to Perpetua's room. They all sat on her floor and picked their way through a variety of strange dishes.

'You know what I should have brought with me,' Perpetua sighed. 'A recipe book!'

'She's right, Bellwin,' Edwin moaned. 'The food here doesn't get any better. In fact, it's got worse. Cockroach dumplings for dinner? That's just gross!'

'He means that's not very nice,' Perpetua explained patiently. She frowned. 'How are Eifus and Dreifus, by the way – has Janus had a word with them about their part in all this?'

'They are with him this very moment,' Bellwin replied. 'They were summoned to the throne room and a servant found them hiding in a laundry cupboard. Eifus was standing between two hanging bed covers, and Dreifus had tried to disguise himself as a pile of towels.'

Perpetua giggled. 'Can't blame them for trying, I suppose.'

'No, but Janus has been true to his word and is laying all blame with Auvlin. Eifus and Dreifus will not be punished.'

Edwin nodded. 'Same with Rownan. Janus told me he wouldn't punish him, either.'

Perpetua sat up. '*I* didn't hear that!'

'He told me in the middle of the night.'

Perpetua screwed up her nose. 'What – he came and woke you up just to tell you that Rownan wasn't in trouble?'

'Sort of.'

'That's a bit odd. Why on earth would he do *that*?'

Edwin told Perpetua and Bellwin about his conversation with Janus, and the king's reaction to Edwin's mention of *Ancient Relics of These Territories*.

Bellwin took a drink of milk, then wiped his mouth on his sleeve. 'The king has always been very secretive about his ancient relics. There is a place in this castle that is forbidden to anyone but him and a few others – I think the relics are kept there.'

'Where *is* this place?' Perpetua asked.

'At the very top of the castle – a little further up than the portrait gallery.'

'But the portrait gallery *is* the top of the castle. There's nowhere else to go.'

Bellwin shook his head. 'This place cannot be seen. It is invisible.'

Edwin frowned. 'So d'you think Janus is worried that Rownan's trying to find this place and get to Janus's relics?'

'Surely not!' Perpetua scoffed. 'That would be like someone with an interest in jewellery trying to break into the Tower of London!' Bellwin looked blank, and she added, 'Our queen's Crown Jewels are in the Tower. *They're* very impressive . . . *she's* a very nice woman . . . Janus would like her.'

'Shut up!' Edwin groaned. 'Let Bellwin answer!'

'We may find out what Janus's concerns are very shortly,' Bellwin replied, keen to avoid a squabble. 'As soon as Rownan arrives back at the lodge, Janus's guards will bring him straight to the throne room.'

'Oh!' Perpetua said, sitting up. 'Are *we* going to be there?'

'Everyone will be there. Janus will speak with Rownan, then he wants to make our plans to deal with the Umbrians.'

Perpetua's eyes widened, and she popped a slice of hog's buttock into her mouth. 'Fantastic,' she said. 'This is starting to get *really* interesting . . .'

Eifus and Dreifus were standing in a corner like a pair of naughty schoolboys. Eifus had his hands clasped behind his back, Dreifus had his clasped in front. As Janus and Auvlin swept into the throne room, the twins edged closer together.

'We will not speak until we are spoken to,' Dreifus announced.

'But you have already spoken *without* being spoken to,' Eifus snapped.

'Brother dear, I merely wished to make our intentions clear.'

'Dear brother, a lengthy silence would have been quite sufficient.'

Janus ignored the twins and nodded to Ollwin, Primus, Lorius and Bellwin.

Edwin nudged Bellwin. 'Where's Mersium?'

'He is away on court business.'

The king sat on his throne and raised his hand; a guard came through the archway, followed by Rownan, who looked tired and unkempt. He glanced around the room, taking in Edwin and Perpetua, then strode to the foot of the steps and bowed.

'Your Majesty . . .' Rownan's tone sounded unsure.

Janus threaded his fingers. 'Where is your son?'

'Back at my lodge. I asked your guards to spare him this ordeal.'

'I see. I understand you have been away – can you tell me where?'

'Yes, sire,' Rownan said nervously. 'My son and I went to see a friend of my late wife. She lives at the western foot of the Blacksaw Hills.'

'And what is her occupation?' Janus asked quickly, as if he were trying to catch Rownan out.

'She is a widow, but she has a smallholding and –'

'Your Majesty . . . Lorius,' Primus cut in. 'I have just been told – and it will interest you to hear – a few of my men were checking the Leigh River dam. On the way back here they passed this woman's cottage . . . Rownan and Mornan *were* there.'

Janus seemed to relax. Edwin knew why – the king had had confirmation that Rownan hadn't been prowling around the castle.

'I hope your trip was worthwhile,' Janus said. He took a moment to think. 'Now – you see that Edwin and Perpetua are here, and will therefore realise my son's plan has been discovered.'

Rownan looked down. 'Yes, sire.'

'I do not intend to punish you for your part. You have been a loyal servant of this court for many years, and I cannot blame any Hysterian for assisting my son.' Janus glanced at Auvlin. 'No matter how misguided his aims.'

Eifus and Dreifus perked up. 'Oh no, sire!' Eifus shouted. 'You cannot blame *anyone*!' He clapped a hand over his mouth.

'I am grateful,' Rownan said to the king. He looked down at his clothes. 'Is that all, Your Majesty – may I go?'

Janus sat forward. 'There is one more thing. There have been sightings in the forest . . . people behaving suspiciously. Have *you* seen anything?'

Perpetua put up her hand. 'But the boy! What about the –'

Ollwin swung round. 'Perpetua! The *king* is speaking.' Perpetua pulled a face and looked down.

Rownan shook his head. It was as if he hadn't even heard Perpetua's outburst. 'No, sire. I have seen nothing.'

Janus smiled. 'Then that will be all, thank you, Rownan. Please go to the kitchens and my cook will prepare you breakfast before you return to your lodge. We will speak again very soon.'

Rownan looked around the room, fixing on Auvlin for a second; then he bowed and walked away. Everyone watched in silence until he disappeared from sight.

'Why didn't you tell him about the boy?' Perpetua said. 'Er, Your Majesty . . .'

'Because the fewer who know what the Umbrians are doing the better. Only those who are *here* should discuss what action we will take.' Janus paused, then looked at Edwin. 'Which brings us to this question, my boy – do you intend to stay in Hysteria?'

Edwin's eyes widened, then he straightened his back. 'Yes,' he said proudly. '*Of course* I'm staying!'

'And me!' Perpetua trilled. All eyes turned on her, and she mumbled, 'If you want me, that is . . .'

'Of course we want you!' Bellwin pulled Edwin and Perpetua into a bear hug. 'It will be just as before!' He let them go and straightened his tunic. 'Except this time I am no longer an apprentice! No more lessons and hours of practice . . . *now* we can –'

'Get straight to work!' Ollwin said. 'Fetch a chair for everyone, Bellwin.'

Edwin and Perpetua helped gather enough chairs, and some servants brought in wine and junoberry cordial.

'I am allowed wine now,' Bellwin said proudly as he sat next to Perpetua.

'I wouldn't touch the stuff if I were you,' she replied tartly. 'Does the brain no good at all. And anyway, isn't it a bit early?'

Janus raised his hand and the room fell silent. He descended the steps in front of his throne, and Primus handed him a map. Janus knelt down and unfolded the large piece of parchment on the floor. Edwin slipped from his chair.

'That's not Hysteria,' he said.

'No,' Janus replied. 'It is Umbria.' He traced a fingertip along a thick black line. 'This is the border with Meticulla – here is the Umbrian fort.' Janus looked up. 'Bellwin – did Brolin show you the place where the transformation took place?'

'Yes,' Bellwin said, crouching down. 'It was in a villa, just here. Brolin told us it was two hours ride from the border.'

'Are we going into Umbria again?' Perpetua asked.

'Yes,' Janus replied. 'As soon as we have agreed a plan of action. And I need to consult Mersium about this area of Umbria – he is due back at court tonight.'

Edwin blinked. 'Are we gonna go to the villa?'

'That is what we need to discuss.' Janus stood up. 'Shall I tell you all what I intend to do?'

Everyone tipped their head.

'I want to go to this villa, enter the underground dungeon and find the poor wretch Brolin spoke about.'

Ollwin frowned. 'And then . . . ?'

'We rescue him and fetch him back to Emporium Castle.'

No one said a word. Ollwin looked at Primus; Primus stared at the floor. Edwin and Perpetua didn't move a muscle.

'Well,' said Janus impatiently, his eyes blazing. 'Has no one *anything* to say?'

'Your Majesty,' Ollwin said carefully. 'Is that course of action wise? An Umbrian living within our walls?'

Janus turned on his heel. 'Have you forgotten, Ollwin, that an Umbrian has lived within these walls for more than twenty years! And when Bellwin told us about this boy, Mersium was the first person that sprang to my mind.'

Ollwin wrung his hands. 'But, sire, Mersium was different. He defected from Umbria . . . he came here of his own free will.'

'And do you think this boy will be happy to stay in Umbria and be *tortured*?' Janus boomed. He began to pace up and down. 'I cannot bear it . . . I could not sleep last night, imagining what pain he suffers.' He stood still, and took a long breath. 'Mersium was only a boy when he came here, and he grew up to be one of my most loyal friends. This young man may prove to be the same . . . to me *and* to my son.'

Edwin sprang to his feet. 'The king's right! We can't just leave the boy in Umbria – he'll end up dead, like the one we found in the forest!'

'Your Majesty,' Ollwin sighed. 'This must be managed very carefully. If we fetch this boy to Emporium Castle, we must assess whether his presence threatens our security. If there is the *slightest* doubt, we will need to think again.' He dabbed at his forehead. 'We should also *try* to transform him back to his former self, to avoid any confusion.' He glanced at Edwin. 'Two Auvlins in Emporium Castle are quite enough.'

Edwin's eyes widened. That meant he wouldn't be going back to being thirteen for a while.

'Excellent!' he hissed.

'Primus,' Janus said. 'What do *you* have to say about this?'

Primus was silent for a moment. 'I have been trying to imagine what Mersium would think. I am sure he would be in favour of your plan, Your Majesty.'

'I agree.'

'Would you ask *him* to go to Umbria, too?' said Perpetua.

'Not necessarily – it would be something of an ordeal after being held captive there. I am tempted to lead the expedition myself, and leave Auvlin here in the care of Mersium, Ollwin and Lorius.'

'Can I come?' Edwin said quickly. 'I'm not afraid to go back, Your Majesty.'

Janus turned to Edwin. He gazed at him, then put a hand on his shoulder. 'I know,' he said. 'You really are a very brave and resourceful young man. *Of course* you may come with us.'

'And me!' Perpetua trilled, grabbing Edwin's arm.

Edwin rolled his eyes, but Janus laughed. 'How could we leave you behind, young lady?' He turned back to the map. 'I will consult Mersium tonight, and we will leave for Umbria tomorrow. Primus – you and your best dozen men will accompany the expedition.' He looked up. 'Ollwin – I would like to take Bellwin with me, as he has been involved in this from the very beginning. He can also perform magic as necessary. Does this meet with your approval?'

Ollwin raised his eyebrows, but he said, 'Yes, sire.'

Bellwin rubbed his hands. 'I will be the expedition magician!'

'*The expedition magician*!' Eifus repeated, jumping up and down. 'What a wonderful rhyme!' He scurried forward. 'And what will *I* be, Your Majesty – the quest guest?'

Edwin whispered, 'How about the trip drip?'

Janus narrowed his eyes. 'You and your brother,' he said to Eifus sternly, 'will stay here in Emporium Castle.'

118

Eifus's face fell, and he scurried backwards. 'To assist in looking after Prince Auvlin,' he murmured. 'Of course, Your Majesty, a very wise decision. We understand entirely. We will not speak until we are spoken to . . .'

Janus rolled up his map. 'You may go . . . our discussions are finished for the time being.'

Lorius and Ollwin bowed to the king, then swept out of the room with Bellwin in tow. Eifus and Dreifus hurried out after them.

'Your Majesty,' Edwin said, pulling Perpetua forward. 'What about us – what can *we* do now?'

'I suggest you each find several more sets of clothes and settle into your rooms. Then perhaps you should have lunch, and look at the history books you studied the last time you were here. It would also be wise to reacquaint yourself with the castle.'

'Can't we help with anything else?' Edwin said. 'You know – your plans and stuff?'

'We will all assemble after I have spoken to Mersium.' Janus looked directly into Edwin's eyes. 'You want to help Hysteria again, my boy,' he said gently, 'and I will not disappoint you.'

CHAPTER TEN

Edwin and Perpetua bundled along the passage towards their rooms. They were loaded down with clothes, and Edwin kept tripping on the uneven stone slabs.

'I wish they'd sort out this floor. I dunno how the servants get on carrying trays and stuff.'

Perpetua slowed down, but didn't answer.

'*I said* I dunno how –'

A face suddenly loomed into view. Long, hollow-cheeked, and lit orange by a flaming torch, Lorius was waiting by Edwin's door.

'Oh! I . . . hello,' Edwin gabbled, ducking behind his pile of clothes.

'Mr Lorius!' Perpetua squeaked. 'It's . . . so . . . nice to see you.'

Lorius narrowed his eyes. 'Is it? If only I could say the same.' He pushed Edwin's door open and jerked his head, signalling them to go inside. Edwin glanced back: what was Lorius so annoyed about?

'What is it?' Edwin said, dumping his clothes on the bed.

'Why did you come to Hysteria?' Lorius asked evenly, closing the door.

'You heard why – for Auvlin,' Perpetua replied. 'He needed help, and Edwin was just the man . . . er, boy to give it!'

Lorius clasped his hands behind his back and rocked on his heels. 'Auvlin needed help,' he repeated slowly. 'He needed help to win a *triathlon* – an event of such importance to Hysteria's standing and security.' His lip curled. 'The vortex is opened . . . valuable resources used . . . court members are distracted from their duties . . . leaving Hysteria vulnerable – just so a competition can be won!'

Edwin folded his arms. 'All that was *Auvlin's* idea . . .'

'Of course it was – but you did not have to agree to it!' Lorius frowned. 'Prince Auvlin has not been his usual self since he was restored to us – particularly after he was treated by Wizard Brolin. And in this altered state of mind, his ideas should not be taken seriously.'

'But I didn't know he wasn't all there! Rownan never mentioned it when he came to fetch me . . .'

Lorius smirked. 'Anyone with a degree of common sense would see Auvlin's plan was ill-advised!' He turned to Perpetua. 'Even *you* wanted to come to Hysteria! Clever Perpetua . . . sensible Perpetua. What made you go along with this ridiculous plan?'

Perpetua blushed.

'*I* can tell you – scientific curiosity.' Lorius turned to Edwin. 'And I know why you came back – to feel *wanted* again . . . to feel *special*. You are not concerned if your actions put Hysteria in peril as long as you return to a hero's welcome!'

Edwin glared at Lorius. 'What's your point?' he growled. 'Just finish what you've got to say and go!'

'The point is,' Lorius replied, 'you must not do anything else that Auvlin asks. Just do as you are told to by Janus.'

Edwin scoffed. 'I don't think Auvlin will ever talk to me again. Did you see him in the throne room? He looked like he wanted to gimme a smack in the mouth!'

'You need not worry about him – the king has asked me to keep a very close watch on our prince.'

Well, at least that might keep Lorius out of Edwin's hair.

'Have you finished now?' he replied coolly.

Lorius held Edwin's stare. 'For the moment.' He took a step forward. 'But one last thing. I would be obliged if you would talk to me with a little more respect.'

Edwin blinked. 'Then don't treat me like I'm Public Enemy Number One!'

They stood nose to nose; Lorius staring down and Edwin looking up. Lorius suddenly turned to go. He sprang the latch and flung the door open.

'Oh, and one last thing,' Edwin called.

Lorius stopped dead and looked back.

Edwin tipped his head. 'Thanks for that A.'

Bellwin had joined Edwin and Perpetua for lunch. Perpetua had hardly drawn breath.

'. . . and *then* Edwin said, "thanks for that A", and you should've seen Lorius's face! He didn't say a word! I almost *died*! I don't know how Edwin plucked up the courage. If he could, I think Lorius would go straight back to Templeton Grove Comp and change that mark to an F!'

Edwin shook his head. 'Make that a Z minus . . .'

'There's no such mark!'

Bellwin crossed his arms. 'Did Lorius ask you about Rownan – about where he had been?'

'No,' Edwin replied. 'It was Janus who was in a tizz about *that*. D'you still think the king's worried that Rownan is trying to get to his ancient relics?'

'Yes, I do. He seemed much happier once Primus

confirmed Rownan had only been visiting a friend.'

'I bet this friend had something to do with the ancient relics,' Perpetua said. 'They took the book, remember?'

Edwin pulled a face. 'D'you reckon they're in some sort of club? I bet their newsletter's a laugh-a-minute! Ancient relic of the month – the arty-farty weird-and-wonderful stone from deepest Oogeywoogeyland, made of pre-historic bogeys and –'

'Edwin!' Bellwin said disapprovingly. 'This is a serious business!'

'I apologise for my friend,' Perpetua said smoothly. 'Bogeys, by the way, are the pieces of mucus that collect in your nose.'

Bellwin's eyes widened and he sniffed.

Perpetua peered at him. 'Don't worry,' she said with a smile. 'You're bogey free!'

Edwin sat forward. 'For goodness sake, Perpetua!' He turned to Bellwin. 'D'you know much about what these relics actually do?'

Bellwin clasped his hands. 'Only as much as is written in *Ancient Relics of These Territories*. You will remember there are lots of relics described as *properties unknown*.'

'I think that sounds a bit shady,' Edwin murmured. 'You'd bet your last pound that *those* ones are used for something 'orrible!'

'Not necessarily,' Bellwin replied. 'Some relics may

be used as a defence, so their properties are best kept secret.'

'D'you think that's the case with Janus?' Perpetua asked. 'Maybe his relics help to defend the castle!'

'Perhaps.' Bellwin sat back as platters of bread and cheese were placed between them. 'What are you doing after lunch?'

'Janus told us to get our bearings again, you know, look around the castle,' Edwin replied; he looked at the table. 'Crikey, Bellwin,' he grimaced. 'What *is* this stuff?'

'It is the closest we can get to your *cheddar cheese*.'

Edwin prodded a bright-orange lump. 'It looks radioactive!'

Perpetua took a breath. 'That's when something exhibits . . .' She paused. 'Bellwin, I *would* explain –'

'But she's gonna get herself a life instead,' Edwin cut in wearily.

Bellwin shook his head. 'No matter.' He took a bite of cheese. 'Oh, that is very tasty! My friends, I have nothing to do this afternoon. Can I join you on your tour of the castle?'

There was one thing Edwin could do much better than Perpetua and that was find his way around. It never failed to amaze him that someone with a sky-high IQ couldn't follow a set of perfectly simple directions.

'Perpetua, you numpty! I said left, left, right. You

went the wrong way . . . AGAIN! I wouldn't mind if you weren't following me.'

'Sorr-y,' Perpetua mumbled. 'I don't tend to keep up with you as much in the daytime. At night it's a *completely different* matter!'

'What? In case the bogey-man gets you?' Edwin scoffed. Bellwin looked rather alarmed, and Edwin added, 'That's not a man made out of bogeys – it's a saying we have in England.'

'It means a very scary person, or a monster,' Perpetua said. 'Right, where are we now, Mastermind?'

'Two floors from the top.' Edwin pointed to a spiral staircase. 'The portrait gallery is up there.'

Perpetua and Bellwin looked at each other, but neither said a word.

'Shall we go up?' Edwin said eventually.

Bellwin hesitated. 'You mean the portrait gallery?'

'Yeah, course,' Edwin replied. 'Let's have a look at some paintings.'

Of course, they all knew what Edwin *really* wanted to do. They all trudged up the stone steps, and when they stood at the entrance to the gallery, Perpetua said, 'I was thinking about this place last night. I wanted to take a closer look at the portrait of the queen . . .'

They all pretended to be very interested in the paintings, but Edwin's footsteps got quicker and quicker as he made his way towards a door at the end of the gallery.

'You lot wanna get yourselves a camera,' he said as he looked at the last portrait. 'It'd save a shed load of time.' He looked around. 'Bellwin, where does that door go?'

Bellwin looked from Perpetua to Edwin, and swallowed. 'I have only ever looked through it once. All I could see was a short passage and a flight of stairs with a dead end.'

'That's got to be the way to the forbidden rooms.'

They all stared at one another, until Edwin blurted, 'Are we gonna have a look, then?'

Bellwin shook his head. 'I am not sure –'

'We haven't got to go any further than the door,' Edwin insisted. 'We can just sneak a peak.'

Bellwin glanced back along the gallery. 'Very quickly,' he said nervously. 'Just a few minutes!'

'I don't know what you're worried about,' Perpetua said. 'I bet it's not even open!' She reached out for the handle and gave it a tug, then squealed as the handle turned and the door swung back.

'You were saying?' Edwin murmured, and he peered through the opening. It was just as Bellwin had described. The passage and stairs were unlit and a stone wall was just visible about four metres up. There was an alcove on the left just before the steps.

'Let's go in . . . just a bit,' Edwin whispered, and he crept through the doorway. The others followed and he edged in a little further.

'It's cold in here,' Perpetua whined, rubbing her arms.

'There must be another exit,' Edwin said. 'Bellwin, where d'you think it is?'

'I do not know,' Bellwin replied, looking up. 'There are no gaps or shutters.'

'Of course there's not!' Perpetua said impatiently. 'It'll all be done with magic.' She turned back to the door. 'I'll close this a bit, just in case.'

But Perpetua spoke a little too late as there was a faint sound from the other end of the gallery.

'Close the door completely!' Edwin hissed.

Perpetua shook her head. 'What if it locks?'

But Edwin leaned past her and pushed the door handle, plunging them into darkness.

'There's an alcove,' he whispered, then turned and began to feel his way along the wall. Once the stone fell away he dived in, pulling Perpetua and Bellwin with him. They stood, chests heaving, and listened to footsteps echo up the gallery towards the door.

'Who is it?' Perpetua whispered.

'Search me,' Edwin replied.

The footsteps kept on coming, growing louder and louder. Then they stopped. Edwin swallowed against the thumping in his throat as the door handle turned.

CHAPTER ELEVEN

Whoever it was, they came into the passage quickly then closed the door. Edwin didn't dare take a look during the few seconds that light crept in. Footsteps scrunched their way past; Edwin held his breath and felt Perpetua's hand brush against his. The footsteps clip-clopped up the stairs, then someone whispered, 'Inveratum.'

Oh, no – it couldn't be any worse – Lorius!

There was a faint tinge of light that gradually grew brighter and brighter; then there was a sudden bang. Perpetua jumped and dug her nails into Edwin's fingers. He winced and bit his lip.

There was a few seconds of silence; Lorius repeated,

'Inveratum,' and once again the passage was in pitch black.

Bellwin dived past Edwin in the direction of the door. He found the handle, but it rattled in his hand.

'It is locked,' he whispered. 'It must lock as soon as anyone enters the forbidden chamber.'

Edwin dragged Bellwin back into the alcove. 'Then we stay here til Lorius comes out!'

All of them kept as still as they could. Edwin's breathing was shaky, and every now and then he heard Perpetua give a little gasp. After what seemed like the longest ten minutes in history Lorius had gone, leaving Edwin, Perpetua and Bellwin slumped against the wall, shaking with relief.

'Oh . . . my . . . God,' Perpetua groaned. 'I thought he was going to catch us.'

'He very nearly did!' Edwin said breathlessly. 'Well, Bellwin, you said only a few people other than Janus could get into this place. We now know who *one* of them is.'

'The king places a great deal of trust in him.'

'Can we get out of here?' Perpetua said impatiently. 'Having a conversation in the dark doesn't seem right!'

'Yeah . . . course,' Edwin replied. 'This time, we can go the other way.'

There was a pause. 'You want to go in *there*?' Perpetua said. She sounded reluctant, but there was no mistaking a hint of curiosity.

'Course! Lorius has been and gone, and he was probably doing something for Janus, so he won't turn up either. Come on, we know the password and everything.'

Edwin couldn't see Perpetua's face, but he was sure it had that should-we-shouldn't-we look.

'But it could get us into all sorts of trouble.' Perpetua sighed. 'Bellwin – what d'you think?'

'It is probably against my better judgement – although Ollwin says I do not have any – but . . . but I think the opportunity may get the better of me.'

'Great!' Edwin said gleefully. 'You go first, Bellwin, you can say the password.'

They all fumbled up to the top of the steps, then reversed back down a few. Bellwin coughed, then murmured, 'Inveratum.'

It all happened very quickly. Within a split second the wall began to disappear, each brick vanishing one by one as if chosen at random by a computer game. Edwin tried to keep up, but his eyes were too slow, and he jumped back as the last stone vanished to the sound of a loud bang. There was a wall of shimmering, shivering mist. Edwin reached out and his fingers disappeared. He felt an icy, tingling sensation, and pulled back his hand. Then, suddenly, the mist dispersed, leaving a hole in the castle wall.

Edwin, Perpetua and Bellwin peered though the opening. There was the quivering outline of a room.

It looked like a hologram, as if its form was being beamed from somewhere far below. They could see through the room's walls and floor and beyond to the rolling fields and hills of Hysteria.

Edwin blinked. 'Bellwin – this can't be seen from outside the castle, can it?'

'No. As I have said before, this place is invisible. So I assume that anyone inside it cannot be seen, too.'

'Incredible,' Perpetua murmured.

Edwin leaned forward to look over the threshold of the passage. The floor of the forbidden room was visible, but so were the stone cobbles hundreds of metres below.

'Who's, er . . . who's going to go in first, then?'

'This was *your* idea,' Perpetua said pointedly. 'So it should be you.'

Edwin gave a half-hearted smile and gingerly lifted his left foot. He scrunched up his eyes as he slowly put it down, then opened them as he felt firm ground beneath his shoe.

'Yeah . . . it's OK!' he yelped, taking another step. As soon as he was in the room, the hologram effect disappeared. Now it looked just like any other room in the castle. 'Come on,' he said. 'It's fine!'

Perpetua and Bellwin followed. 'Goodness,' she whispered. 'How on earth do they do it?'

'Like you said before,' Edwin replied. 'It's magic!' He looked around; there was no furniture, and no decorations adorned the walls, only another door. 'There's nothing to see in here,' Edwin said. 'Let's see if there's another room.'

He crept forward and turned the door's handle. He inched it open, but suddenly caught his breath and stepped back.

'What is it?' said Perpetua, rushing forward.

Bellwin looked over her shoulder and exclaimed, 'By Janus!'

The last thing they expected to see was a person sitting on the floor – not least a beautiful young woman wearing what looked like a toga and nothing much else. The woman looked up. Her bright blue eyes widened only a little – she didn't look at all scared or surprised.

'Greetings,' she said. 'Who are you?'

Edwin looked at Bellwin, then passed through the doorway. 'My name is Ed – er, Auvlin.'

The woman looked at Bellwin. 'And you?'

'My name –'

'Should we be telling her this?' Perpetua cut in. 'She might –'

The woman held up her hand. 'I am bound never to reveal who visits me here, and never to repeat any conversation that passes between these walls.'

'That's a result!' Edwin hissed.

Bellwin pushed past Edwin and knelt down by the woman. 'Why? Is all that passes here secret, my lady? Do you work with the ancient relics?'

'Yes. My pledge ensures their safety and that of those who instruct me. It has been so since my incarceration began.'

Perpetua stepped into the room. 'Incarceration. *Are* you a prisoner?'

'No, my lady. I am a free Hysterian, but my work keeps me hidden away.'

'How long have you had this job?'

'Over two thousand years.'

Edwin almost choked. The woman's eyes, her skin, her lustrous brown hair . . . there was nothing to say that she was more than nineteen or twenty. 'I'm sorry,' he said, 'but how *can* you be that old?'

The woman smiled. 'Time does not touch me in this room. I am here . . . but I am *not* here.' She picked up a hand mirror that lay by her side and looked into it. 'I observe our king's ancient relics, and in return I retain the beauty of my youth.'

Perpetua put her hands on her hips. 'But what's the point of *that*? No one will ever see it.'

'*I* see it,' the woman replied. 'As long as I am here I can look upon my face, knowing it will never age.'

'But you'll never *do* anything else . . . you'll never *go* anywhere else.' Perpetua shook her head. 'I'd rather turn grey and enjoy myself.'

The woman put down the mirror. 'That is *your* choice, my lady.' She looked up. 'I ask again – what are your names?'

Edwin coughed. 'I might as well be up front. My name's actually Edwin.'

'My name is Bellwin.'

'And I'm Perpetua. What's *your* name?'

'You may call me Saleena.'

Edwin looked around the room. 'Where are the relics?'

'They are here . . . and they are not here.'

'Can we see them?' Bellwin asked. 'Can we touch them?'

Saleena gazed at Bellwin, then she held out her hand. Bellwin frowned, and Saleena said, 'Touch it.'

Bellwin hesitated, then reached out. But his fingers didn't meet hers, instead they passed through the vision of her skin, as if their hands were merging. Bellwin gasped and quickly withdrew.

Saleena smiled. 'I am here . . . and I am not here. The relics are here . . . and they are not here.'

Bellwin blinked and looked at his hand. 'So the magic keeps them safe, beyond the reach of *anyone*. And you, too.'

Edwin took a deep breath. 'I think I need to sit down.' He flopped onto the floor and the others joined him. After a while, Bellwin was the first to speak.

'How many ancient relics does Janus possess?'

'Two.'

'Can you tell us what they do?'

'One preserves the magical auras of Emporium Castle.'

'How does it do that?'

'That I cannot tell you.'

Edwin coughed. 'What does the other one do?'

'It guards Hysteria's crystal mines.'

'How does it do that?'

'That I cannot tell you.' Saleena smiled again. 'I sometimes hear it at work, far away in the mines . . . but that is all.'

Perpetua leaned forward. 'What do you hear?'

'The sound of hissing.'

Perpetua pulled a face, and mumbled, 'That doesn't give much away.'

'So what I have heard must be true,' Bellwin said to the others. 'Only a few in Hysteria know how the relics work.' He looked at Saleena. 'You said your role here is to observe the relics. What do you mean?'

'I listen . . . and tell my visitors of any activity.'

Edwin chanced his arm. 'And the visitors are . . . ?'

'That I cannot tell you.'

Edwin nodded. 'So you said.' He narrowed his eyes. 'You had a visitor a little while ago, didn't you?'

'Yes.'

'And was there anything to report?'

'That I cannot tell you.'

Edwin glanced at Perpetua. 'Well, at least we know she won't grass us up!'

'Are you expecting anyone again soon?' Perpetua asked.

'That I cannot tell you.'

Perpetua got to her feet. 'We're not getting very far here. I think that's a cue to make our exit.'

Edwin looked at Saleena. She had picked up her hand mirror again and touched a gold brooch that was pinned to her toga. 'Have you got anything else to tell us?' he said.

Saleena didn't look at him. 'No.'

Edwin glanced around. What must it be like to be stuck here, day after day, *century after century*, with only your reflection for company? Looking good couldn't feel *that* great. 'You're right, Perpetua,' he said. 'It's time to go.'

Bellwin followed Edwin and Perpetua to the door, but before he passed through he said, 'I wish you well. Goodbye.'

Saleena didn't answer. Bellwin walked into the other room and whispered the password. The wall fell away and Edwin and Perpetua stepped through.

'How sad,' Bellwin said as he joined them. 'How very, very sad.'

CHAPTER TWELVE

Edwin held his breath as he reached for the door back into the portrait gallery. When the handle turned he groaned, 'Crikey, that's a relief.'

'You know,' Perpetua said as they walked towards the stairwell. 'I've seen some amazing things here, but that room just might top the lot.'

'You'd have to go a long way to beat it,' Edwin agreed.

'I am curious,' Bellwin said thoughtfully. 'Why would the ancient relic that guards the mines make a hissing sound?'

Edwin shrugged. 'Er . . . maybe it makes a door swish back and forth.'

'I don't think so,' Perpetua answered. 'A hissing sound would be produced by something like hydraulics – and Hysterians don't use that sort of thing.' She sniffed. 'I won't bore you with an explanation, Bellwin.'

'Do you remember what Janus said when he caught us at the lodge,' Bellwin said. 'That there have been some strange incidents at the mines? That must be how they know – Saleena tells them of any activity.'

'But Janus didn't say any crystals had been taken,' Edwin pointed out. 'So the relic must be doing its job.'

Bellwin shrugged, then turned to Edwin and Perpetua with a smile. 'Then we will think about it no longer. Mersium returns this evening and we will *all* be dining with the king!'

Thankfully, radioactive cheese wasn't on the menu that night. Edwin and Perpetua sat down to roast venison and buttered vegetables, followed by the most delicious lemon cream pie. Mersium arrived halfway through the meal, and Janus and Auvlin left the table to talk to him alone. It was almost an hour before they came back.

'As you can see, Mersium,' Janus said as he sat down, 'Edwin still bears a remarkable resemblance to our prince.'

Mersium took a seat and looked from Edwin to Perpetua. 'It is good to see you both again. At least circumstances are not as grave as the last time.'

'Has Janus told you *everything*?' Edwin almost whispered.

Auvlin lowered his head, but Mersium looked around the table. 'Yes,' he said. 'What the king proposes is right. We must know for certain what the Umbrians are doing, and we cannot stand by and let what may be an innocent boy come to further harm.'

Ollwin cleared his throat. 'Then, Mersium, we must hope the Umbrian we bring to Emporium Castle is as honourable as you.'

Mersium scraped back his hair. 'If it becomes clear this boy is our enemy, I will be happy to deal with him.'

'So,' Janus said, 'Mersium, Primus and I are in agreement. Lorius – what do you think?'

'We must act,' Lorius replied. 'By taking this boy we will surely delay the Umbrians' plans. And he will undoubtedly provide useful information.'

Mersium took a gulp of wine, then looked across the table at Auvlin. 'How do you feel about this, Your Royal Highness?'

Auvlin barely looked up. 'I do not favour this expedition,' he said bluntly. He looked at Janus. 'Do not go,' he said, although his voice was strangely flat. 'Please, do not go.'

Mersium sighed. 'It has to be done, Auvlin. Your plan may have been ill-conceived, but it has exposed something we would otherwise know nothing about.'

Auvlin didn't reply and just stared at the table. That

remark didn't seem to make him feel any better.

'Do not worry,' Ollwin said, patting his hand. 'As Mersium says, your father would be in greater danger had your plan *not* been discovered.'

Auvlin whipped his hand away and sprang to his feet. He glared around the table, as if he was going to say something, but instead he wheeled about and strode out of the room. Two soldiers who were standing at the archway marched after him.

'Is he gonna be all right?' Edwin asked.

'We must leave him,' Janus said. 'I will see my son later this evening. The guards will watch over him until then.'

'Guards?' Perpetua said.

'A precaution to ensure his safety at all times. He has protested, of course, but I will leave nothing to chance.' Janus took a deep breath. 'Now, Mersium tells me this villa is within a region that is sparsely patrolled, so the dozen men that Primus and I have chosen to accompany us will be ample protection. We will cross the Umbrian border at the closest possible point to the villa – my spies have provided a detailed map of the area.'

'Are we going to wear some sort of disguise?' Edwin asked.

'Cloaks,' Primus replied, 'for anonymity. When Janus and I chased you that night in the forest, you had no idea we were Hysterians.'

Edwin swallowed at the memory. 'And is it OK that I look like Auvlin?'

Janus half-smiled. 'Let me say this – it will be no hindrance.'

Edwin hadn't felt so excited in ages. He got up very early and tried on all his new clothes. He wanted something that made him look more like Mersium, or Primus. He went for all black. What would be the point of going on an expedition like *this* wearing pale blue tights?

'Goodness me!' Perpetua trilled when she breezed into his room without knocking. 'You look like the Grim Reaper!'

Edwin looked at Perpetua's gold tunic and scoffed. 'What d'you wanna wear *that* for? D'you wanna say, "Here I am standing out like a sore thumb. Come and get me!"'

Perpetua looked down. 'Mmm . . . I suppose you're right. But you can't blame a girl for wanting to look *nice*.'

After breakfast Perpetua changed, then they both went to meet everyone in the stable yard. While their horses were made ready, Bellwin took them to one side of the yard and pointed up.

'Look there – right at the top, to the left of the uppermost window,' he whispered. '*That* is where the forbidden rooms are.'

Edwin shielded his eyes. 'Crikey! You can't see a thing.'

'To think she's up there,' Perpetua added. 'It's like she's sitting on thin air . . .'

Edwin felt a hand squeeze his shoulder. 'Ouch!' He tried to pull away, but could only strain to see who was behind him.

'What are you looking at?' Lorius said slowly.

'We're looking . . . up . . . there . . .' was all Edwin could answer.

'I could see that. *What* are you looking at up there?'

'It was –'

'Shut up!' Lorius snarled at Perpetua. 'I asked Edwin.'

Edwin swallowed. He looked past Lorius to Perpetua. She made flapping motions with her hands.

'It was a bird!' Edwin spluttered. 'Bellwin,' he added hopefully, 'what was it called again?'

'The Greater Crested Greeb,' Bellwin answered, quick as a flash. He tapped Lorius's arm. 'A pair nested at the top of the castle, last summer. Do you not remember?'

'I have no interest in wildlife,' Lorius snapped. 'Just make sure that is *all* you are interested in.'

They all watched Lorius stride away.

'That *really* hurt,' Edwin whined, rubbing his shoulder.

Soon everyone was mounted and ready to go. They'd

all been given a replica of a chain and amulet that Agnetha has used to get into the Umbrian villa. Mersium stood with Lorius at the stableyard gate, and Janus shook their hands in turn.

'Look after my son while I am gone,' he said last of all to Mersium. 'I have insisted his guards remain for the time being. Do not let him persuade you otherwise.'

'Do not worry, sire,' Mersium replied. 'He is safe with us.'

Janus raised his hand and the gate was opened. 'Edwin,' he called, 'come and ride with me.'

Edwin trotted forward on Spur and they led the procession towards the castle's huge wooden doors. As they swung open, Janus looked at Edwin and smiled.

'The last time you rode out of Emporium Castle, my heart burned because I could not go with you. Now we ride side by side.'

Edwin swallowed. He wanted to reach out and grab Janus's hand but instead he said, 'Don't you wish Auvlin was with you?'

Janus looked down at his reins. 'It would not be safe, Edwin. And . . . and I do not think my son would *want* to accompany me.'

Edwin shook his head. 'Only because he thinks what we're doing is dangerous. He doesn't want *you* to go to Umbria – he said so last night! He's worried something'll happen to you.'

'Things have not been the same, Edwin, since –'

'No, Your Majesty,' Edwin blurted. 'He's worried about you! He loves you!'

Janus seemed to blink away a tear. 'I am sure you are right . . .' He looked behind him. 'Ah, Primus, come and join me. I wish to discuss our route to Umbria.'

Edwin let his horse fall back to ride beside Bellwin. 'Why doesn't Auvlin realise what he's got?' he mumbled. 'I'd do anything to have a dad like that.'

The expedition had crossed the border over two hours ago. The shadows had faded and there was now a chill in the air. Primus led the line of horses through the gathering dusk towards the edge of a forest.

'There can't be far to go now,' Edwin said.

'No, the villa is very close,' Primus answered. He kicked his horse forward. 'The clearing is nearly upon us, sire. Once we leave the forest we will –'

But Primus suddenly pulled his reins, then shouted back, 'Lieutenant, take your men out of sight!' He turned to Janus. 'Two Umbrians are approaching. They have seen *us*, but I am sure our men were too far back. We –'

'Wait!' Edwin said. He took a second to recover from hearing his own decisive voice. 'Primus and Bellwin – take down your hoods and put your weapons on show. Pretend you're Umbrians. Me, Janus and Perpetua are your prisoners – right?' He hid his hands under his cloak. 'Do this and look down. Don't say a word! Like we saw in the forest . . .'

Edwin kept his head down and listened to the sound of approaching horses.

'What is your business?' a deep voice said eventually.

'Prisoners,' Primus replied. 'Bound for the other side of the fort.'

There was the jangle of riding tack, and Edwin felt the flank of a horse press against his leg. Someone tried to look into the shadow of his hood.

'Who are they?'

Edwin's recoiled from a waft of bad breath.

'One thinks he's the king of Hysteria!' Primus guffawed.

The man prodded Perpetua's leg. 'And this one – a female? What did she do?'

'Stealing bread to feed her brothers and sisters.'

The rider's horse swung around. 'Mad men and thieves!' he cried. 'If I had my way I would hang them all!'

There was silence. Edwin swallowed hard. What if the man asked them to pull back their hoods? Edwin was desperate to raise his head and see what was going on. Finally, the Umbrian's horse wheeled around again. 'Water,' he shouted to Primus. 'Give me your water!'

Now Edwin couldn't resist looking up – all their water bottles were marked with a faint Hysterian crest.

What if the Umbrian noticed? Primus reached for his bottle, and handed it over with the crest facing away. The man put it to his lips; he tipped it up, closing his eyes just as the crest came into full view. He took what seemed like an eternity to drink, then took the bottle from his lips and frowned. He shook his head. Edwin's heart was in his mouth.

'Where is the regulation bottle?' the man demanded. 'This is too small for a long journey.'

'Mine was lost,' Primus replied casually. 'This was all I was given.'

Edwin held his breath as the Umbrian examined the bottle again. He turned it over, but his thumb covered the crest. 'Then ask for another,' the man snarled, thrusting the bottle back to Primus. 'Be on your way!'

The Umbrian and his companion disappeared into the forest. After a few minutes, Primus's men came trotting through the trees.

'They have gone, my lord,' said the lieutenant.

Bellwin grasped Edwin's arm. 'That was very quick thinking, my friend.'

Primus pulled up his hood. 'We must not risk another encounter like that. We need to reach the villa as soon as we can. Follow me towards the next line of trees.'

The party trotted into open land but this time they stuck close together. Twenty minutes later Primus spotted lights and very soon the Umbrian villa came into view. It was smaller than Edwin had imagined. It had very few windows, and thick black smoked spiralled from two chimneys.

Primus ordered his men to retreat behind a thicket, and Janus gave everyone a chain and amulet. Edwin squinted in the half-light, tracing the outline of a wax seal with his finger.

'So this is like the one Brolin's friend used?'

'I hope so,' Janus replied, putting his over his head. 'Or our expedition will come to a very abrupt end.'

Perpetua looked at the remaining chain in Janus's hand. 'Who's the other amulet for?'

'The boy – I have a cloak for him, too.'

'What about the guards,' Edwin asked. 'How will they know if we need them?'

'I will use magic,' Bellwin reassured him. 'I need only utter a few words and a sign will appear to them.'

Their horses were led silently away, and Janus slid his sword out of sight.

'Pull up your hoods, everyone. Make sure your amulets are fully displayed.' He turned and walked towards the villa. Primus and Edwin were at his shoulder; Perpetua and Bellwin followed.

'You know,' Perpetua said, her voice quivering slightly. 'I'm not sure I want to do this, now . . .'

CHAPTER THIRTEEN

It was too late for any second thoughts. As they approached the villa, a man stepped outside a large wooden door and stared at them.

'Stand your ground, everyone,' Janus said calmly. 'Try not to let him see our faces – the seals should be enough to let us through.'

As they came closer, the man took a long sword from under his cloak and held it so its tip rested between his boots.

'I have my blade at the ready, sire,' Primus whispered.

But as Janus walked into torchlight, the man squinted at the pendant.

'You bear the mark,' he grunted, and turned to tap

three times on the wooden door. He checked both Janus and Edwin's amulets, but didn't bother with Primus, Perpetua or Bellwin. There was the grating of metal then the doors slowly opened.

Janus nodded and passed through into a dark entrance hall with a lone torch barely flickering from a sconce on the wall.

'Straight ahead,' Bellwin whispered, and Janus led the way towards another pale-orange glow. It grew colder as they walked deeper into the villa.

Bellwin issued instructions in a low, calm voice. 'There will be a stairwell on the left.'

Suddenly, a woman came round a corner towards them. She was struggling to carry a large glass jar filled with clear liquid. Floating in the liquid, its soft tissue swaying delicately, was what looked like raw meat.

Perpetua stopped. 'Is that –'

'Don't!' Edwin pulled her arm. 'We haven't got time.'

Janus found the stairwell. The steps were damp, and Edwin pulled his cloak tight around him as they climbed further and further down. The next floor was even darker than the first. Two men who were talking intently appeared from a side passage and brushed past Janus to climb the stairs. The oldest of the two suddenly stopped and grabbed Primus's arm.

'Which order are you with?' he demanded.

Primus lifted his pendant. 'We arrived tonight.'

The man peered at the seal, then nodded and continued his climb.

When he was out of sight, Edwin whispered, 'These pendants are blimmin' brilliant!'

Janus put a finger to his lips and frowned at Edwin, who mouthed an apology.

'Where now, Bellwin?' Janus murmured.

'The second passage to the right. Through a stone archway – look for a wooden door at the very end.'

The passage leading to the wooden door was lined with portraits, and the faces that looked out from them were the sort to stop anyone in their tracks. Some were of men, some were of women. Some were young, some were old. But they all had the same look – pale skin; a thin, cruel line to the mouth; and the sort of stare that was almost alive, as if a real person was there behind the image, just waiting for you to turn your back.

'Are these the Umbrian wizards?' Perpetua murmured, peering at the pictures.

'I think we can be sure of that,' Janus replied.

'Will there be any of them in the villa now?'

'Undoubtedly.'

'Then can we get a move on?' Edwin muttered.

Janus put his hand on the door and pushed it open a little way. He peered in, then turned back. 'It is safe to enter.'

When they were all inside, Perpetua closed the door behind her. The room was hexagonal, and at the centre was what looked like an examination table. Beside the table was a stone plinth and resting on its top, glinting in the soft torchlight, were several metal instruments.

Primus picked one up. He moved a metal shaft and a sharp point sprang forward.

'Barbarians,' he hissed, showing it to everyone. 'Who knows what they use *this* for.'

But Edwin and Perpetua had noticed some shelves high up along one wall, lined with the kind of large glass jar they'd seen the woman carrying a few minutes earlier.

While the others were deep in conversation, Perpetua scurried forward and put a wooden box under the shelves. 'What is it in these jars?' she whispered, stepping up. 'Is . . . is it human remains?' She paused. 'Oh, goodness, yes . . . heart and lungs – probably a child's.'

Edwin made a gagging noise. Perpetua teetered to the right.

'Intestines in here – they've been cut about a bit . . .'

'Oh, please,' Edwin pulled a face and pointed to the left. 'What about there,' he said quietly, trying not to disturb the others. 'There's a jar with some white balls in it.'

Perpetua moved her box along a bit, quickly jumped back on it and pulled a glass jar towards her. 'Eyes,' she said bluntly. 'They're eyes!'

Edwin felt the pit of his stomach lurch. 'Ugh . . .' he moaned.

'They're not like normal eyes,' Perpetua added, leaning forward. She beckoned her friend over.

Edwin plucked up courage and joined Perpetua on the wooden box. He peered at the glass jar. There were several eyes floating in the liquid, each one trailing a pink and white cord.

'What are the long things?' Edwin asked queasily.

'The optic nerve, of course,' Perpetua replied. 'More importantly,' she added, 'none of them appear to have an iris. It's like they've all been blanked out.'

Edwin glanced at her in admiration. They'd been to all the same science classes but he'd never even heard of an optic nerve.

But before he could ask her any more, the others finished talking.

'Come down, quickly,' Janus said impatiently. 'We must find the boy.'

Edwin and Perpetua climbed down from the box and followed Janus towards a door. 'Primus – stand guard,' he said. 'You know what to do if anyone enters.'

Janus opened the door out onto another set of damp steps. They led down to a dark and dingy passageway that was lined with cells.

They began to walk along the passage. The first cell they came across was small and barely lit, but it was possible to make out ten or twelve children sitting between its four walls. They weren't identical, but they all looked very similar. Were they all from the same family, Edwin wondered? He frowned. Why were they just staring straight ahead? And they were so quiet – not even the tiniest sound came from any of them.

'What . . . what *is* this?' Edwin mumbled, 'Why are they . . . ?'

'Keep going, my boy,' Janus said gently, moving on.

But Edwin walked to the bars of the opposite cell. About the same number of children sat together on a thin blanket of straw. Again, they all looked alike. And *again* there was no movement at all, and not so much as a whisper or a grunt. Edwin put his hand through the bars. If he tapped one of the boys on the shoulder, would he look at him?

The nearest boy caught site of Edwin's hand and shrank back. He lost his balance, fell to one side and came face to face with one of the others. Suddenly the boy started to scream; he stared at his cellmate, seemingly in horror, and wailed. The noise filled the air. It echoed along the passage, distorting wildy. It was too loud. *Too loud . . .*

Edwin's stomach lurched. Someone would hear! The Umbrians would discover them! Edwin tugged at the bars. They were locked fast. He looked around in panic. He had to stop the noise before –

'Bellwin,' Janus said loudly over the screaming. 'Open the gate!'

Bellwin stepped forward and said, 'Revernum!' There was a clank and Janus swung the gate open, stepped inside the cell and grabbed the boy, his hand clamped over his mouth. The wailing carried on, muffled this time, but as soon as Janus dragged the boy away from his cellmate it stopped.

'What was it?' Perpetua said. 'He didn't seem to want to look at the other boy . . .'

'We do not have time to find out,' Janus replied, gently putting the breathless boy back on the floor. 'We need to act more swiftly than ever.' He stepped out of the cell, locked the gate then strode down the passage, looking quickly from side to side. Everyone followed him. The next cell was the same as the others. And then the next. Four, five, six cells, and then . . .

The last cell had only one occupant. He sat on a bench, his head down. His long brown hair was matted and dirty, his black gown was covered in stains.

Janus put his hands on the bars and whispered, 'Hello?'

The boy looked up, alarmed. He slid further along the bench and sat cowering against the far wall. His face was thin and his eyes were dull and bleary but there was no mistaking who he resembled. The boy looked exactly like Auvlin. Exactly like Edwin.

'It is him,' Janus murmured. He shook his head. 'Bellwin, unlock the gate.'

Bellwin pushed to the front, held out his hand and

said, 'Revernum'. Within seconds the gate swung open. The boy stood up, stumbling to his left, clearly terrified.

'We will not hurt you,' Janus said gently, pulling back his hood.

The boy stared back, and said nothing. Janus reached out, and the boy's gaze flickered down to Janus's hands.

'Do not be afraid,' the king said softly. The boy's ragged breathing steadied. He looked as if he might burst into tears, then his eyes closed and he sank to the floor.

'He's fainted!' Perpetua rushed forward and lifted the boy's head. 'Get some water – quickly!'

A bottle was produced and a trickle of water splashed onto the boy's lips. He opened his eyes and focused on Janus. He let out a whimper.

'Can you stand?' Janus asked.

'We are here to rescue you,' Bellwin said gently. He helped the boy to his feet. Janus passed Bellwin the cloak and it was wrapped around the boy's shoulders.

'Put this on,' Janus murmured, and he produced the sixth amulet. The boy groaned and tried to push it away, but Janus held his hand.

'You must. We are *all* wearing them,' he whispered, then gestured for Edwin to hold his pendant to the light. 'They will help us escape. Once we're away from this place we can take them off.'

The boy nodded weakly and the pendant was put in place, then Janus gently led him out.

'What about the others?' Edwin hissed.

Janus shook his head sadly. 'We cannot take them all.'

Bellwin peered into a cell. 'Edwin, I . . . I do not think they have any sense of where they are, or what is happening. I fear it is too late for them. '

Janus pulled the Auvlin lookalike close to him. 'We must take the one who *is* aware.' He walked along the passage, then carried the boy up the steps and through the door.

Primus swung around and helped Janus steady the boy on his feet.

'You need to walk out of the villa with us,' the king said gently. 'Can you do that?'

Bellwin led the way. This time they didn't see a soul, and within a few minutes they were back at the front door. Janus and Primus walked either side of the boy as he limped into the evening air.

'Thank you,' Janus said, tipping his head at the guard. 'We are much obliged.'

CHAPTER FOURTEEN

They arrived back at Emporium Castle as the sun was rising. Everyone grabbed a few hours sleep, and in the afternoon they were all summoned to the throne room.

'The boy is very tired, and still a little scared,' Janus began. 'But Ollwin and I have spoken to him.'

'What did he say?' Edwin asked eagerly.

Janus shook his head. 'Nothing. My physician thinks he is unable to speak . . . for the moment.'

'It's probably because of what the Umbrians did to him,' Perpetua said. 'Some sort of trauma.'

'So you don't even know his name?' Edwin said.

'I know only one thing – I asked if he would like to go back to his original form, and he answered with a nod.'

Janus looked at Ollwin. 'What do you think? How long would it take?'

'According to Brolin's notes, only a few minutes,' Ollwin replied. 'The change back is much faster than the initial transformation, because the subject already has all the information needed within his or her body.'

'Oh, yes!' Perpetua trilled. 'Brolin told us all about this. Anyone who's transformed always keeps one of their own physiological features.'

'Yes, exactly right.'

Perpetua's eyes glinted. 'Do you know how all the information is contained?' she added. 'On Earth, we call it the double helix. It's a –'

'Stop showing off!' Edwin moaned. 'We haven't got all day.'

'Perhaps later, my dear Perpetua,' Ollwin said gently. 'Your Majesty, we should make the change soon – it would be ill-advised to wait.'

'But hold on,' Perpetua said slowly. 'If you're transforming him from one image to another, isn't that . . . *Shadow Magic*?'

Ollwin shook his head. 'We will be *reversing* a Shadow Magic spell, therefore strictly speaking we would still be acting within the bounds of Ancient Magical Lore.'

Everyone looked at Janus. He nodded. 'Very well, Ollwin,' he said gravely. 'Lead the way to the boy. We will reverse the transformation without delay.'

The room was dimly lit and they found the boy half-asleep. Ollwin turned up the light and the boy awoke. He was slightly hesitant but didn't look petrified, as he'd done when they'd found him in the Umbrian villa. Janus sat on his bed.

'Hello, young man. How are you?' The boy gave no response. 'I would like to introduce some other people,' continued Janus. 'This is Ollwin. He is Hysteria's High Wizard.'

Ollwin nodded and stepped forward, but the boy edged back on the bed.

'Do not be afraid,' Ollwin said softly. 'Hysterian wizards practice *white* magic. I will do you no harm.'

Janus glanced at Edwin. 'This is my son, Prince Auvlin.'

Edwin shook his head vigorously.

'The young lady is Perpetua,' Janus continued, 'a distant cousin to our family. Bellwin here is also a wizard.'

'Yes, I am!' Bellwin said proudly. The boy gave a faint smile.

'Now,' Janus continued, seeming pleased to have made some progress. 'I asked if you wanted to be transformed back into your original form and you indicated that you would.' The boy looked from Janus to Ollwin and back again, then nodded.

Janus laid a hand on the boy's arm. 'Would you like us to do it now?'

The boy frowned, then his bottom lip began to quiver. Ollwin sat on his other side. 'I am sure it will not be like before, my friend,' he said softly. 'It should take no time at all. Before you know it, you will be just as you were.'

The boy looked down hesitantly, then nodded again.

'Very well,' Ollwin said. 'It is probably best if you lie down.'

Perpetua scurried over to hold the boy's hand, pushing a pillow under his head. 'He's shaking. Don't worry . . . don't worry,' she whispered to him.

Ollwin stood up and took some notes from his pocket. 'Now,' he said gently. 'I will first cast my own white magic spell, then repeat the words of the transformation spell. While I do this, I will place my hand upon your chest – the magic needs to find the part of your body that has retained all the information about your original form. It is from *this* that we may change you back. Do you understand?'

The boy nodded and gripped Perpetua's fingers.

'Very well, I will begin.' Ollwin held out his hand. 'Revernum colloquia spell elaborata –' He laid it on the boy's chest. '– transalish verflesh morbotten elaborata.'

Almost at once Ollwin's hand seemed to be sucked down, and a split second later the boy screwed up his eyes and let out a low cry. Ollwin removed his hand, and the boy's head began to turn rapidly from side to side, his breathing shallow and shaky. He suddenly stiffened and arched his back. Ollwin put his fingers under the boy's wrist.

'His pulse is not too fast. He appears to be in no pain.' He stepped away from the bed. 'Give him room, Perpetua.'

Edwin drew up a chair. 'He looks a bit sweaty,' he murmured.

'That is to be expected,' Ollwin replied.

Edwin watched, his mouth gradually gaping open. The boy was changing before his very eyes. His hair turned from brown to blonde, shrinking from shoulder length to fall just below the jaw. The face changed, moulding slightly higher cheekbones and a more pointed chin. The boy's skin grew paler, and what were long fingers became a little more stubby.

'Listen to me!' the boy shouted suddenly, making everyone jump. His arms jerked, then started to shake. His brow creased. 'This is the last child we can use for now . . .' he whispered. 'Crystals are running low . . . we may have to consider using the prisoner . . .'

'What is wrong with him, Ollwin?' Janus asked anxiously. 'Is this to be expected?'

'It seems to be some sort of delirium,' Ollwin replied. He checked the boy's pulse again. 'I do not think he is in any danger, sire.'

'But what is it he's going on about?' Edwin said. '*This child* . . . who was *this child*?'

Ollwin frowned. 'Perhaps others in the Umbrian cells?'

'Perhaps he was repeating something,' Bellwin said. 'It takes weeks to complete transformation once the initial spell has been cast . . . he may have overheard many conversations subconsciously.'

The boy suddenly put his hands to his head. 'More experiments,' he said. 'Are you sure the villa is secure?' He flopped his arms back onto the bed. 'We are running out of crystals . . . RUNNING OUT . . .' He shivered violently, then all of a sudden he stopped and fell into a still, calm sleep. Now, lying there, he looked like a completely different boy, and two or three years younger.

'Blimey,' Edwin whispered. 'That was *amazing*.' He shrugged. 'Well, at least we know he can talk.'

'Mmm,' Perpetua agreed, folding her arms. 'Shame it made no sense at all.' She folded her arms and looked at Ollwin. 'But one good thing – if Bellwin's right and the boy is just repeating what he's heard, it sounds as if the Umbrians are still low on crystals.'

Janus ushered everyone out, saying that they had a lot to discuss. Perpetua tugged on Edwin's sleeve and grinned.

'Did you see Ollwin's face? He's happier already!'

But only ten minutes later Perpetua was glaring around the throne room with her hands on her hips.

'You're going to let the triathlon go ahead? You're still going to let Edwin compete? But aren't there more important things to deal with?'

Edwin looked at Perpetua, shaking his head. 'Why don't you let Mersium and Janus finish?' he sighed. 'Stop interrupting everyone and just chill out!'

Perpetua glanced back at Edwin, then blinked and lowered her hands. 'He means I should try to take a more relaxed attitude,' she said stiffly.

Ollwin surpressed a smile. 'I agree, we should remain calm.' He turned to Primus. 'My lord, what do you think of Mersium's suggestion?'

'He is right,' Primus answered. 'If we postpone the competition the Umbrians may realise we know about their activities. If we carry on as normal we will have more time to get to the bottom of their plans. We have the boy, he may yet tell us something *vital*.'

Mersium sat forward. 'How do you feel about this, Edwin? Would you still be willing to compete in the triathlon?'

Edwin studied Mersium for a moment and decided he was a lot like Janus. They both wanted to protect Hysteria, but first they wanted to be sure that Edwin was happy with their plans. Edwin glanced at Primus, now *he* –

'Do not worry, Edwin,' Primus said, jumping to his feet. 'We will ensure your safety at all times. I will do everything in my power to protect you, just as before!'

Janus gestured for Primus to sit down, then winked at Edwin. 'Do you need time to think about this, my boy?'

Edwin smiled and shook his head. 'Nah, course not! I was *always* gonna compete and now it's even better, because all of you are here to help me. It's not just Bellwin, and Eifus and Dreifus . . . you're all on the case!'

Perpetua threaded her fingers. 'He means you're all involved in the situation.'

'Auvlin will be pleased,' Edwin said. 'He didn't want the competition to go ahead without him, and now it won't. Sort of . . .'

'You mean it will not go ahead without *you*,' Janus corrected him. 'I will not let my son through the castle gates until it is clear the Umbrian threat has been defeated.'

Perpetua frowned. 'If Edwin takes his place won't *he* be in danger?'

'No, Perpetua. Thousands of people attend, so he will be quite safe.'

'But what about the orienteering?' Edwin asked carefully. 'I'll be running around on my own.'

'Once again there will be no danger. Hundreds of elite guards from all territories are posted throughout the forest for the protection of all the royal competitors. They are highly trained soldiers – the Umbrians are very unlikely to risk taking them on.'

'That's a result!' Suddenly, Edwin felt quite excited.

He stood up. 'Now, I'd better get to work with Rownan again. Orienteering *is* the first trial, isn't it? I've lost track of time . . . how long have we got 'til it starts?'

'Less than a week,' Bellwin replied.

'But what else has Edwin got to do?' Perpetua asked. 'What do the other disciplines involve?'

Janus cleared his throat. 'Horse riding . . .'

Great, Edwin thought. Those lessons at home had really payed off.

'. . . and wrestling.'

Edwin's face fell. He hadn't even seen the WWF on television. He eyed Perpetua.

'Don't look at me,' was all she said.

'Thanks a bunch.' The only thing Edwin could think of was people prancing around wearing patterned leotards pretending to knock each other senseless. He turned to Janus. 'Is there a . . . uniform?'

Janus nodded. 'Your triathlon clothes are fitting for a Prince of Hysteria.'

Edwin half-smiled and tried to lose the image of a leotard with a crest on it.

Janus had arranged for Rownan to come to the castle that evening after dinner so Edwin could continue his lessons. The time came, but Rownan was late. Eventually he hurried in. He had a book in his hand and was scribbling notes in the margin.

'Everything all right?' Edwin enquired, craning his neck to see what the woodsman had written.

'Yes, Edwin,' Rownan said quickly, shutting his book. 'Now, we must go over what you learned in our last lesson.' He unravelled a map. 'I have to tell you,' he added grumpily. 'I thought your studies would stop when Auvlin's plan was discovered.'

Perpetua raised her eyebrows at Edwin. 'You sound like you'd much rather be doing something else, Rownan,' she said lightly.

'Perhaps so, Perpetua, but the king's orders cannot be ignored.'

Edwin got to work, and it soon became clear that he hadn't forgotten anything Rownan had taught him. So they pushed ahead with areas that they hadn't covered yet.

'I know this is way out of the orienteering area, but if I kept going north where would I end up?' Edwin asked, tracing his finger across an unfamiliar area of the map.

Rownan squinted. 'All that area is farmland . . . it is known as the Greenacre Valley. But the land rises steeply *here* and is used only for grazing.'

'And these are the . . .' Edwin peered at the tiny writing. 'The Blacksaw Hills?'

'Yes – they are the second highest point in the territories, only the Balgarian mountains – over here – are higher.'

'So does anyone live in the hills?'

'The land is very rugged. Not many people settle – it is hard to make a living.'

Perpetua plonked her chin on an upturned palm. 'You went to the Blacksaw Hills, didn't you? When you went away with your son?'

Rownan hesitated, but didn't look up. 'Yes, we did.'

'You went to see a friend of your wife's . . . I remember you telling Janus in the throne room. You said she was a widow and that she had a smallholding.' Perpetua frowned. 'Why does she live there on her own, if it's tough to get by?'

Rownan cleared her throat. 'Her husband gave Hysteria long and good service. Agnetha –' Rownan stopped for a moment, before adding quickly, 'She is well provided for by Janus.'

Edwin and Perpetua glanced at each other – he'd said *Agnetha*.

Rownan sighed heavily. He'd obviously had enough of this conversation. 'Now, Edwin – we should go back to the western edge of the forest. Do you remember where the mines were situated?'

An hour later when Edwin announced he'd had enough, Rownan didn't hesitate to pack away. He left the room with his bag slung over his shoulder and dug into his pocket for the book he'd been making notes in earlier.

'I don't think I've ever seen anyone less enthusiastic to be anywhere,' Perpetua said pointedly as she closed the door. 'It reminded me of when I did that presentation on gravity . . . Nat looked at his watch so many times I thought he'd lost his short-term memory!'

'D'you know *why* Nat did that?' Edwin said, putting his hands behind his head and swinging backwards on his chair.

Perpetua shrugged.

'Because it was BORING!'

Perpetua sighed and sat down. 'Nat Parker thinks anything that doesn't involve a bouncy rubber sphere is a waste of time,' she said huffily. 'At least *you're* bit more open-minded.'

'Mind how you go,' Edwin replied, grinning. 'That was almost another compliment.' He sat up straight. 'So, the widow that Rownan and Mornan went to see is called Agnetha . . .'

Perpetua eyes glinted. 'Oh, yes! It's got to be the same woman, don't you think?'

'Course it is. I haven't come across any two people here who are called the same thing. It's not like home – there's so many Chloes and Jessicas in our year it must be a nightmare for the teachers.'

'You're the only *Edwin* I know,' Perpetua pointed out. She creased her nose. 'Why did your parents call you that? It's so old-fashioned! Your brother and sisters' names are really quite normal.'

'I've asked them,' Edwin sighed. 'My mum's explanation is *weird*. She said when I was born she didn't have a clue what to call me. But the morning after, in hospital, when she took me out of my cot, she said she noticed something different about my eyes . . . and, for no reason at all, the name Edwin popped into her head. My dad didn't like it, but Mum said that was what it had to be.' He looked up. 'Anyway . . . get *you* calling "Edwin" old fashioned! Where did Professor and Lady Allbright get *your* name from?'

Perpetua stuck her nose in the air. 'It's taken from the word *perpetual*, which means –'

'Yeah – I do know! It means going on and on all the time . . . always up and running,' Edwin guffawed. 'Blimey, they were spot on!'

'Yes, they were!' Perpetua replied proudly. 'Now, we're getting off the point – does the fact that Rownan knows Brolin's friend have any significance?'

Edwin shrugged. His head was so full of stuff he couldn't even begin to work it out. 'Don't ask me,' he said. 'You're supposed to be the clever one!'

CHAPTER FIFTEEN

Perpetua spent the next morning in the library, while Edwin had more lessons with Rownan. When he broke for lunch he went to get Perpetua, and found Bellwin had joined her to tidy up the books.

'I told Ollwin *before* that this place was a mess,' Perpetua said impatiently. 'And it hasn't been touched. Look!' She pointed to a pile of books on a table. 'They've been there all this time. Nine months!'

Bellwin scratched his head. 'How do you *know* that, Perpetua?'

'Because I brought a book back the morning we left, and I saw Eifus dump those on the table – on the exact same spot! He was about to put them on the shelves, but then Dreifus opened the door and started shouting . . .' Perpetua started to laugh. 'He . . . he had porridge all over his head, and he was holding a ladle with some more in it. Dreifus told Eifus to come out, because . . . because he didn't want to ruin any books!'

Edwin grinned. 'Wicked! A porridge fight!'

'Yes,' Perpetua said weakly. 'I got away as fast as I could!'

Edwin walked over to the table and ran a finger down the succession of spines. *'Brothers: Friends or Enemies*? . . . *A Guide to Family Rivalry* . . .' He let out a cackle. 'This is a good one: *How to Leave your Sibling*.'

'Eifus didn't learn anything, then,' Perpetua said. 'They're still together!' She looked around. 'Er, Bellwin, I meant to ask you. Can you find *Ancient Relics of These Territories* for me? You said there was a copy here?'

'Yes, of course. It should be on those shelves . . .'

Bellwin was back very quickly.

'Thanks,' Perpetua said. She took the book and put it in her pocket. 'I'll have a look at that later.' She looked towards the library door, then leant forward. 'You know, Bellwin, we have something to tell you. Yesterday, Rownan told us the widow he visited when he was away was called Agnetha. Edwin and I think it *must* be the woman who is friends with Brolin.'

Bellwin thought for a moment. 'Rownan volunteered this woman's name? He did not try to keep it a secret?'

'Well, I think he let it slip by accident more than anything else,' Perpetua said. 'He doesn't give much away, so surely if she were some dark and deadly secret, he'd make sure her name was *never* mentioned.'

'Yes,' Bellwin agreed. 'And Primus said some of his troops had seen Rownan and Mornan at this woman's cottage. The king's intelligence services are very good so if Rownan meeting Agnetha was a threat to Hysteria, Janus would know.

'Rownan did say this woman was a friend of her late wife . . . perhaps the interest between them was a family matter.'

'Yes, it could've been anything,' Perpetua replied. She frowned. 'I wonder what her husband did? Last night Rownan made him sound quite important.'

'I am sure I can find out!'

'Great! I was also wondering –'

'Perpetua!' Edwin moaned, grabbing his stomach. 'I'm starving! Can we please get something to eat! Bellwin, are you gonna come with us?'

'I have already eaten,' Bellwin replied. 'There is an errand I must perform, then I will try to find out about Agnetha's late husband.' He led the way to the door. 'You may enjoy lunch today! I believe the cooks have tried to . . .'

But Bellwin's words fell away as the door swung open – Lorius was standing in the passage. All three instinctively edged closer together.

'Oh, hello!' Perpetua squeaked.

'Good afternoon,' Lorius said quickly. 'You three look very busy. Where are you going?'

'Me and Perpetua are gonna get some lunch,' Edwin replied, trying to sound defiant. 'Then she's sitting in on my afternoon lesson with Rownan.'

'I have to collect a new batch of crystals for Ollwin,' Bellwin added. 'And then . . . and then I am not quite sure . . .'

Lorius's gaze flicked to Edwin. Edwin made sure his eyes didn't drop.

'I have something very important to tell you,' Lorius said finally. 'You must all keep to your rooms tonight, from after dinner for the duration of one hour. You are strictly forbidden to enter any other area of the castle.' He looked back to Bellwin. 'It is the ceremony . . . I would be grateful if you would reassure Edwin and Perpetua that there is no danger. These are Janus's orders, naturally.'

'Yes, Lorius,' Bellwin replied.

'Thank you.' Lorius pushed past Bellwin and looked into the library. After staring inside for a few seconds, he turned and stalked away. As soon as he was out of sight, Edwin turned to Bellwin.

'Ceremony?'

'Yes. The miner's ceremony, strangely enough. But do not worry – as Lorius said, we will all be quite safe.' Bellwin swallowed. 'I am glad you waited until he had gone before you asked me that . . . Lorius likes people to know as little as possible.' He shoved his hands in his pockets. 'Now, I really do have to go. I will try to see you later today.'

'OK,' Edwin replied. He and Perpetua walked away down the corridor. Edwin suddenly swung around to say something to Bellwin, but he'd disappeared from sight. 'Oh, no!' Edwin wailed. 'He's gone!'

'What on Earth's the matter?' Perpetua said grabbing Edwin's arm. 'Is something wrong?'

Edwin sighed and shook his head. 'Yeah . . . he was gonna tell us what was for lunch!'

'Which bright spark told them I like mashed-up tomato?' Edwin said ten minutes later, spooning a red lumpy mixture around a large bowl.

'I think that might have been Bellwin,' Perpetua replied carefully. 'He probably meant to say tomato ketchup, but got it wrong.'

'Great! And he also didn't mention it's a sauce . . . you put just a *little bit* on a sausage sarnie, or on fish and chips. Not a whacking great splurge of the stuff and nothing else!'

Perpetua didn't eat it either, but they both went to the kitchen and managed to cadge a radioactive cheese sandwich and a huge piece of cake to eat during Edwin's lesson.

The lesson turned out to be a long one, and neither of them realised how late it was when they finished and went in search of Bellwin.

'I bet he's still in the library,' Perpetua said.

She was right. They found Bellwin in the middle of a pile of dusty books, leafing through something that looked familiar.

'That's the court record!' Perpetua said, sitting next to him. 'Is it the edition we looked at last time?'

'Yes, it is. The king ordered the recording of court activity be resumed as soon as Auvlin returned to us. I have often looked at the day after he awoke. Your names are recorded, too!' He flicked through some pages. 'Look!'

Edwin grinned. 'Excellent! Just before we went home. So, have you found out anything about Agnetha's husband?'

'Yes,' Bellwin replied. 'I was just trying to verify something.'

'What have you found out so far?'

'Well, it seems that Grettel – that was his name – had a very important role. If I am right he was, in fact, the Master Miner.'

Perpetua stared at Bellwin. 'So what's that, then?'

'The Master Miner is in charge of all the men who work in the crystal mines. Not only that, it is also his responsibility to make sure that his men are initiated and renewed by the ceremony . . .'

'The thing that's going to happen tonight?' Edwin said quickly.

'Yes, the very same.' Bellwin looked back at the court record. 'I must just check something. I stayed in the castle the night before Ollwin started me as his apprentice. I remember that everyone was confined to their rooms and I wondered what all the secrecy was about.' He ran a finger down a page. 'Yes, here we are – Grettel was at the castle on the very same date. He *must* have been the Master Miner and was here to perform his duties.' Bellwin looked up. 'You know, there are pictures of all the Master Miners in the portrait gallery.'

Perpetua shot to her feet. 'Really? They might give us some clues about what this secret ceremony involves . . . I'd love to find out! Let's go and have a look!'

Edwin, Perpetua and Bellwin had all forgotten Lorius's instructions about the time as they made their way up to the portrait gallery. They climbed the last steps then hurried along the cold stone floor, each scouring the walls.

'Where exactly are these paintings?' Perpetua asked Bellwin.

'They are not together,' he replied. 'They are hung apart. The small metal plaques at the bottom will tell us who the subjects are.'

'*Lady Mordread Evershold*,' Perpetua said, squinting in the half-light. 'Oh, she doesn't look very nice . . ..'

'And she *sounds* like a right laugh,' Edwin added flatly, moving on. '*Antonine of Antoninum*. Have you seen the size of this guy's nose?'

They carried on down the line, until Perpetua suddenly said, 'Look – he's here!'

Edwin and Bellwin scurried over to join her. The portrait showed a man in his fifties. He was dressed in fine clothes and a dark blue sash, and in the palm of his left hand rested a large but slightly mottled crystal. A table was in front of the man, and on it was a small axe.

'He looks very important,' Perpetua said wistfully. 'And that is one *big* crystal he's holding!'

'It looks as if it has been freshly dug from the mines,' Bellwin replied 'I should think it symbolises the Master Miner's work.'

Perpetua narrowed her eyes. 'There's an outline of something in the background . . . what is it?' She pointed.

Edwin leant towards the painting. 'Can't tell. It's a bit too dark.'

Bellwin pushed past them. 'There is the vague shape of a circle . . . and something in the middle that appears to glint slightly.' He stood back. 'It is very hard to tell for certain.'

Perpetua glanced around. 'Where are the portraits of the other Master Miners?' she said. 'Let's see if the same thing is there.'

Sure enough, they saw the same faint outline with a hint of sparkle in the background of three more paintings.

'You can tell a bit more from this one,' Edwin murmured, almost pressing his nose to a portrait of someone called Dresius Finkerjingle. He stepped back. 'But it's like the others . . . still not very clear.'

'Well, perhaps we should consider the axe?' Bellwin said. 'Does it –'

But Perpetua suddenly grabbed his arm. 'Shhhh!' she hissed. 'I can hear something!'

Sure enough there was the sound of footsteps coming up the staircase at the far end of the gallery. Edwin looked around, grabbed Perpetua and Bellwin and dragged them behind a huge landscape painting that was leaning against a wall. They crouched in the darkened triangle of space, peaking through the gap at the other end. After a few seconds Lorius and Janus came into view, then another man wearing a silk tunic and a dark blue sash, with a small axe that swung back and forth from his thick leather belt.

'He's dressed like Grettel in the portrait,' Perpetua whispered, peering past Edwin. 'He must be the current Master Miner.'

'Blimey,' Edwin muttered, 'the ceremony . . .'

They all watched as a line of men followed Janus, Lorius and the Master Miner along the gallery. Edwin counted about twenty of them. They were all blindfolded. Edwin held his breath as the line filed past their hiding place, then watched Janus approach the far end of the room.

'The door to the forbidden chamber!' Bellwin blurted.

'Sshhh!' Edwin and Perpetua wagged their fingers at him.

Janus opened the door, and it wasn't long before the last of the men disappeared from sight and the door was closed. There was a lengthy silence, then a muffled bang.

'The wall's come down,' Edwin said, letting his voice rise above a whisper. 'Did you know they did the ceremony in *there*, Bellwin?'

'Of course not.'

'I wonder what part Saleena plays?' Perpetua turned to Bellwin. 'It's going to take about an hour. Can we risk making a run for it?'

'I do not think so,' he replied, shaking his head. 'If I were caught, I *dread* to think what my punishment would be.'

Edwin pulled a face. 'Don't suppose *we'd* be flavour of the month either . . .'

'He means we wouldn't be very popular,' Perpetua sighed, then added, 'So why are the men wearing blindfolds?'

'Both the ceremony and the forbidden chamber are secret,' Bellwin replied. 'The blindfolds must be to help keep them that way.' He closed his eyes. 'How could we have possibly forgotten about the ceremony?'

'Well, it's no use thinking about that now,' Perpetua said. 'We've just got to stick it out here until we think it's safe. If we come across someone later, we'll say we've only just left our rooms.'

They spent what felt like a long time in the cramped space behind the painting, speculating about what was going on in the forbidden chamber. What was the ceremony? Was Saleena conferring some honour on the men, like the Queen of England? What exactly did the Master Miner do? Did Janus or Lorius give out the orders?

Eventually the door at the end of the room opened, and Janus emerged from the gloom. Lorius and the Master Miner were next, followed by the line of men, who were still blindfolded. The first of the men had his hand on the Master Miner's shoulder, the second man had his hand on the shoulder of the first, and so on and so on. Edwin shuddered – it looked like black and white film of wounded soldiers in the First World War.

The procession made its way back down the gallery, and soon the sound of muffled footsteps faded away to nothing. The children decided to wait a while before venturing back out into the room. They began to breathe more easily once they were well away from the gallery staircase. But they were stopped in their tracks when they suddenly saw Ollwin coming towards them. All three fixed a smile.

'Master!' Bellwin said stiffly. 'How are you?'

Ollwin frowned back at him. 'I am well.' He looked at Edwin and Perpetua. 'I was just coming to see you – the Umbrian boy has spoken at last, and the king would like us all to visit him in the morning.' He put his hands behind his back. 'May I ask where you have been?'

'We haven't *been* anywhere,' Perpetua gushed. 'We're just *going* to the library.'

'Yeah,' Edwin added. 'We've just come out of our rooms . . . we stayed in them for an hour after dinner, just like Lorius said we should.' He felt himself flush red. 'Dinner was *really* nice. It was, er . . .'

Perpetua yanked Edwin's hand. 'I'm sure Ollwin's not interested in what we had for our evening meal!' she trilled. 'I'm sure he's got lots of important stuff to do.' She moved away and jerked her head at the boys. 'Have a nice evening, Ollwin. See you in the morning!'

When they turned a corner, Perpetua crossed her arms. 'Honestly, Edwin! How daft are you? When you tell a bare-faced lie on the hop you need to keep it as brief as possible. That was too much information!'

'Sorry,' Edwin muttered. He looked at Bellwin, not quite sure where to begin. 'Er . . . she means –'

But Bellwin shook his head. 'Edwin,' he said grandly, 'I understand!'

CHAPTER SIXTEEN

The next morning Janus summoned everyone to visit the Umbrian boy. Edwin followed the king into the room and found the boy looking much brighter.

'Good day, my friend,' Janus said warmly. 'How are you?'

The boy looked from one person to the next. He opened his mouth slightly, hesitated, then said, 'I am will.'

Perpetua giggled and sat down next to him. 'You mean you're well! Don't worry, you're probably still a bit confused.' She put a hand on the boy's forehead and his eyes widened. 'But you're right! No temperature . . . and you look *so* much better!'

'No, no,' the boy insisted. 'I am Will. It is my name.'

Edwin sighed and rolled his eyes. 'Sorry about that,' he said wearily. 'She's like that *all* the time.'

Will smiled, but looked at Janus. 'When you asked me my name, I wanted to tell you, but . . . but I could not.'

'It is a blessing to hear it at last!' Janus replied. 'Perpetua is right – you look very well. Have you eaten?'

'Yes, I had a very good breakfast.'

'I hope they didn't try him with the ketchup,' Edwin said aside.

'I am glad that you have eaten well,' Janus said. 'And you are rested?'

'I do not think I have ever slept for so long in my life,' Will replied. But then he looked down. 'Except at the villa – when I was changed.' He quickly raised his head. 'I want to help you, King Janus. For as long as I can remember, I was told the Hysterians were my enemy and that you were a cruel and angry people.' He looked around. 'But everyone has been so kind . . . not like the Umbrian wizards. They did nothing but hurt me.'

Ollwin walked forward. 'Were you *taken* to the villa, Will, or had you always lived there?

'I was taken from my family, just before my last birthday. There were others who had been taken from their homes too. Friends of mine. The wizards took them to the chamber one by one, and I never saw them again . . . I was the last.' Will wrung his hands. 'But I was told there were other boys who had always been at the villa. I saw them. They were strange.'

'How so?' Janus asked gently.

'They did not speak . . . I did not ever see or hear *any* of them do *anything*. It was if they did not have their own thoughts.'

'We saw young men like that when we rescued you,' Janus said.

'I would say something to them, but they would not reply – they would not look at me.' Will frowned. 'Or one another. I was once kept chained outside a cell for hours and I watched the boys inside. They seemed to even avoid each other's eyes.'

Edwin nodded. 'We saw the same thing . . .'

Perpetua edged forward. 'D'you remember much about when you were in the chamber? You know, while the Umbrian's magic was working?'

'No, nothing.'

'I ask because when Ollwin was reversing the spell, you were talking quite a lot. But you seemed to be repeating things that the Umbrian wizards had said.'

Will looked quite startled, but said, 'I am sorry – I do not remember anything.'

Janus glanced at Edwin, then back at the boy. 'Are you aware of *who* you looked like after the Umbrians had cast their spell?'

When Will didn't reply, Edwin said, 'You looked like *me*.'

Will blinked. 'But you are the king's son,' he said slowly. 'You are Prince Auvlin.'

Edwin nodded quickly. 'Yes, I am.'

'Do you know *why* they made you look like Auvlin?' Ollwin asked. 'It would help us a great deal if we knew.'

Will shook his head, looking confused.

Janus sat down on Will's bed. 'But you are here with us, and I am glad of it,' he said. 'If you wish to stay, we will take care of you.'

'It's great here!' Perpetua said cheerily. 'You'll like it!'

Will's chin began to tremble. 'May I?' he said, gazing at Janus. 'May I stay in Hysteria?'

The king grasped his shoulder. 'Many years ago, another young Umbrian came to Hysteria and asked me to give him shelter.' He turned to the doorway where Mersium was standing, his eyes shining.

'That boy,' Janus continued, 'grew up to be the most loyal friend I could wish for. He has honoured this kingdom and repaid me a thousand-fold. If another Umbrian wishes to follow in his footsteps, how can I refuse?'

Mersium came and stood beside Janus. 'There is no better place to make your home,' he said to Will. 'And no better monarch to serve.'

'Are *you* Mersium?' Will asked.

'Yes,' Mersium replied. 'And now your fellow Hysterian.'

Edwin swallowed against a lump in his throat. He leant forward and shook Will's hand. 'Wicked!' he croaked. 'Er, I mean welcome . . .'

Will grinned. 'Thank you, Auvlin.' His hand froze. 'But should I call you "Prince Auvlin"?' He turned to Janus. 'And what should I call *you*?'

Ollwin clapped his hands. 'It seems that lessons in court etiquette are required!' He looked knowingly at Edwin and Perpetua. 'It is not too long since they were last provided!'

Janus looked up. 'When would Eifus and Dreifus be able to commence lessons?'

'I do not think they are busy,' Ollwin replied flatly. 'They merely spend their time trying to keep out of everyone's way.'

'Then I will tell them myself that they have a new charge,' Janus said, getting to his feet. 'Let us leave our young friend for now. Quickly – before we tire him.'

Janus walked with Edwin and Perpetua while everyone else went their own way. The king told Edwin he was to have a swordsmanship session that afternoon with him and Primus.

'I have asked Auvlin to join us – it would be wise for you to adopt something of his style.'

'Oh . . . OK,' Edwin muttered, not quite sure about spending time with Auvlin.

'How exciting!' Perpetua trilled. 'Can I come? Can I have a go?'

But Janus gave a sorry smile. 'I am afraid, my dear, that other arrangements have been made for you.'

'What arrangements?' Perpetua said nervously, remembering last year's private lesson on how to stuff a chicken.

'Tournament etiquette,' Janus replied. 'There are certain traditions that ladies of the court must follow.'

Perpetua's face dropped. 'Did you say *etiquette*?'

'Yes. For example, each lady must favour one competitor and demonstrate their support in certain ways.'

'What, like waving a hanky around?' Edwin said with a smirk. 'Do me a favour, Perpetua and don't wave yours at me – I've seen you blow your nose in it!'

'Etiquette,' Perpetua said again. 'That sounds like . . .'

'An Eifus and Dreifus production!' Edwin cackled. 'Brilliant!'

Perpetua spent the whole of lunchtime moaning about having to face an afternoon with the Gonks. They came to collect her. Dreifus greeted her with a deep bow and Eifus produced a red silk handkerchief from his pocket.

'For your use, my lady,' he said with a toothy grin.

'See? I was right,' Edwin said smugly.

'And what do I do with it?' Perpetua asked through gritted teeth, hoping that the answer might prove Edwin wrong.

Eifus extended his arm, like a prima ballerina. 'You hold it thus,' he said softly. 'It flutters in the breeze and . . .' He shook the handkerchief gently, and something fell to the floor. Everyone looked down at a gungy yellow lump.

Eifus turned on Dreifus. 'Dear brother,' he spat, 'I have asked you many times not to clean out your ears with my best silk kerchiefs!'

Dreifus darted forward and tried to kick the lump of earwax under the table, but it stuck to his boot. 'I am sorry, brother dear,' he mumbled, picking it off with his fingers. 'It was all I could find this morning.' He added in a whisper, 'The toilet closet had run out of paper.'

Eifus turned back to Perpetua. 'My deepest apologies,' he gushed, offering the handkerchief. 'Please, my lady . . . you must become accustomed to holding it.'

Perpetua looked at Edwin and grimaced. He raised his eyebrows and sighed, 'The loo was out of paper. It coulda been worse . . .'

Perpetua swallowed, took the silk square between her thumb and a fingertip and muttered, 'Let's go.'

Edwin couldn't help smirking every now and again about Perpetua as he practised sword fighting with Primus. He'd picked up where he'd left off pretty quickly, and Janus was impressed. Auvlin, however, said nothing. He stood and watched stony-faced.

'Good, my friend,' Primus said after half an hour, lowering his sword. 'Well done. Now, you should watch me practise with Auvlin. The movement of his wrist is a little different to yours – you must try to imitate it . . . others may notice on the day of the sword-fighting discipline.'

Auvlin stepped forward reluctantly. 'My arm hurts,' he mumbled. He rolled up his sleeve to show a purple bruise.

Janus was at his side in an instant. 'How did it happen? Did somebody hurt you?'

'No, father,' Auvlin replied, sounding irritated. 'I . . . I hurt it on a stable door two days ago. It is nothing . . . it is just uncomfortable.'

Primus examined the bruise, then resumed his position. 'We will practise for only a few minutes,' he said. 'Just enough so that Edwin may see your style.'

Auvlin gave a grudging nod and held up his sword. His blade flashed against Primus's, but his stance looked awkward. The swords clashed and ran against each other. Auvlin grimaced and held his arm.

'You *are* in pain,' Janus said gently.

'Did you not believe me, father?' Auvlin snapped. He looked down and dug the tip of his blade into brown dust.

'Of course, my boy,' Janus replied. He looked at Primus. 'Auvlin must see my physician. I will take –'

'The pain will ease on its own,' Auvlin interrupted. 'I will see no physician.'

Janus hesitated, but then nodded. 'As you like, but if the pain worsens I am afraid I will have to insist.' He put his hands behind his back. 'Perhaps we should take the opportunity to tell you what we have decided regarding the triathlon.'

'That is obvious, father – Edwin is to compete on my behalf in all disciplines.' Auvlin smirked. 'From what I have seen, I do not think Hysteria's prince will win in swordsmanship this year.'

Edwin let his sword drop. What was it with Auvlin – why did he seem to bear such a grudge?

'Oi!' Edwin snapped. 'I've only done this a few times. *And* I'm doing you a favour. I didn't have to come here – it was you that asked me, remember!'

'Apologise, Auvlin!' Janus demanded. 'Both Edwin and Perpetua took a great risk in returning to Hysteria – at *your* request.'

Auvlin looked down and swallowed. 'Forgive me, Edwin,' he said, as if trying to inject a little warmth into his voice. 'My . . . my father has told me I have not been myself for some time, and I fear it is true.'

Edwin sighed, trying to remind himself what Auvlin had been through. 'That's all right,' he replied. 'We'll work things out – don't worry.'

'May I go now?' Auvlin said dismissively, his couldn't-be-bothered tone returning.

'Yes,' Janus said, taking his arm. 'I will walk you to your guards.'

Auvlin yanked his wrist away. 'Yes, back to my guards! I am nothing more than a prisoner, father . . .'

Edwin watched the king and his son walk from the courtyard. Auvlin was different from how he'd expected.

'There goes one very unhappy bunny,' Edwin sighed. He glanced at Primus. 'That means Auvlin's a bit miffed.' He frowned. 'That means he's –'

'It is not important,' Primus said firmly. He raised his sword again and gestured for Edwin to do the same. '*This* is!'

'Blimey, Auvlin is soooo ungrateful!' Perpetua screeched at Edwin later that night. They were sitting with Bellwin in front of the fire in the dining hall. 'I'd like to see him come to Templeton Grove Comprehensive and sit a chemistry exam for me. He'd probably set a new record for the lowest ever test score!'

Edwin stuck a finger in the air. 'Not possible.'

'Why?'

'I already hold it and it's one record that *can't* be broken.'

Perpetua's eyes widened. 'You mean you got –'

'A big fat zero!'

Perpetua glanced at Bellwin, sat in shocked silence for a few seconds, then said, 'Logic tells us there's nothing big or fat about a zero. It's nothing. It doesn't exist.'

Edwin sighed. 'Well, Einstein, it certainly existed at the top of my test paper.' He huffed. 'I bet *you've* had a couple of big fat zeros in your time . . . with a lil'old one right in front of 'em!' He looked at her. 'Am I right?'

Perpetua fiddled with her dress. 'Yes . . . I, er, happen to have got one hundred per cent in exams before,' she admitted. But she soon recovered herself. 'Bellwin, that means that I achieved full marks.'

'You must be very clever,' Bellwin replied, his eyes full of admiration. 'I wish *I* were as able as you.'

'Don't be silly,' Perpetua replied. She reached across and adjusted Bellwin's collar. '*You* passed the most important test of all – Full Wizarding. And what a time to do it . . . just in time to help defeat the Umbrians!'

When Bellwin blushed, Perpetua looked away. 'Now,' she added, 'I want to ask you some questions.' She reached into a bag that was lying on the hearth and pulled out the library copy of *Ancient Relics of these Territories*. 'I've managed to remember some of the relics that Rownan and Mornan had marked and I just wondered if you knew anything more about them.' She opened the book. 'Here's one – the "Niosin Amulet". It says it's a grey flatweave stone on a twisted silver chain, and that it was made in Hysteria. D'you think *that* might be one of the relics in Janus's possession?'

Bellwin peered at the drawing. 'Just because it was made here it does not mean it will still *be* here. They are ancient, after all, anything could have happened to them over the thousands of years that have gone by.'

'Yes, I suppose so,' Perpetua agreed. She turned to the next page, and read, 'The Armegia Charm from the Eastern Lands. A yellow Balgarian crystal cast in metallic Jura. Now, Bellwin, from what —'

'That's a familiar shape,' Edwin butted in, over Perpetua's shoulder. 'I might be wrong, but it's a bit like the thing in the background of the Master Miner paintings . . .'

Perpetua gasped.

'Oh, yes!' She scoured the drawing, then shoved the book under Bellwin's nose. 'What d'you think?'

Bellwin took his time to look. 'It is very much like the one featured in the paintings.'

Perpetua shut the book and clutched it to her chest. 'Can we go to the gallery and have another look?'

Edwin shook his head. 'I don't wanna risk being caught up there for a while. We only *just* got away with being out of our rooms while the ceremony was going on.'

'Oh, well,' Perpetua said breezily. 'Perhaps I can show you *this*.' She dug around in her bag again and produced a slim leather-bound book.

'What is it?' Edwin asked.

'Well,' Perpetua said grandly. 'I was trying to find something about the management of the vortex – I asked Lorius, but he wouldn't tell me anything – then I came across this in the library.' She held the book up.

'*Traditions and Ceremonies of the Hysterian Court*,' Bellwin read. 'Where did you find it? I did not even know it existed!'

'It was tucked away at the back of a dusty old shelf,' Perpetua replied proudly. 'It felt like a prize find when I read the title!'

'OK, Sherlock,' Edwin said. 'And what did you find inside?'

Perpetua looked at Bellwin. 'He's referring to one of *our* fictional characters called Sherlock Holmes – he solves the deepest, most baffling mysteries with a process of simple logical thought.' She smiled smugly. 'He's a genius!'

Edwin gritted his teeth. Perpetua was on the brink of becoming unbearable. 'Yeah, yeah, yeah,' he moaned. 'I wish I'd kept my gob shut now. Just get on with it!'

Perpetua looked down and turned a page. 'Hmmm . . . well,' she said. 'I scanned the whole book, but I couldn't find anything specific to the secret ceremony. That's not a surprise, of course – it's a secret!' She pointed to a paragraph. 'But this bit *does* talk about traditions and ceremonies that are carried out in the castle and "are known to only a few Hysterians". Beside this paragraph someone has scribbled something . . . and *that's* the interesting bit.'

Edwin and Bellwin peered at the faint scrawl of writing.

'It took a bit of working out,' Perpetua continued. 'But it says "MMG omitted one with grave consequences". The way it's written, it's like a reminder . . . something that was meant to be removed later, but was forgotten.' Perpetua looked up, her eyes gleaming. 'What d'you make of it?'

'MMG – could that be a name?' Edwin said. He looked at Bellwin. 'There are people here with one or two names, but is there anyone with *three*?'

'Not that I know of,' Bellwin said. 'It would be very unusual.'

'Then the MMG must be something else,' Edwin shrugged. Perhaps it wasn't in the least significant. Trust Perpetua to make something out of nothing.

'Well, perhaps I can have a think about it during my next lesson with Eifus and Dreifus,' Perpetua said. 'Because it's not worth listening to anything *they* say!'

Edwin sat forward. 'You didn't tell me what happened. Come on, spill the beans!'

Perpetua crossed her hands. 'He means tell him everything, Bellwin.' She shook her head. 'You're going to have to wait until the triathlon, Edwin. I'm not going to embarrass myself showing you what they taught me about tournament etiquette until it's absolutely necessary.'

Edwin rubbed his hands together. 'Brilliant! What I wouldn't give for a video camera. Can't wait . . . I *can't wait*!'

CHAPTER SEVENTEEN

Edwin had a few days to wait. Not that he wasn't kept busy in the meantime. He had several more lessons with Rownan and continued to practise swordsmanship with Primus. But he also had a disastrous tutorial in wrestling. 'Less said about that the better,' he told Perpetua. 'I don't think my performance is gonna do much for Auvlin's street cred.'

The morning that the triathlon began the castle was bustling with activity. The huge tents and seating areas had been set up the day before, but now servants rushed around with food and drink and the royal horses were being groomed to within an inch of their lives. Just before noon six elite guards rode alongside

Edwin and Perpetua to the starting point for the orienteering contest. Rownan was waiting for them, and he and Edwin went over some last minute points.

'If I get stuck can I come and find you?' Edwin asked anxiously.

'If you get lost,' Perpetua butted in before Rownan could reply, 'you might not be able to find *him*, either!'

'I am sorry but I am not able to stay for the competition,' Rownan replied.

'Oh,' Edwin said, a bit deflated. 'Why?' He'd been counting on the woodsman's support.

'My son is unwell,' Rownan said quickly. 'I must attend to him.'

Edwin and Perpetua looked at each other, but before they could ask what was wrong, Rownan continued, 'You will not need my assistance, Edwin, I am sure of it. You need only do your best to have a chance of winning.' He slung his bag over his shoulder and offered Edwin his hand. 'I have enjoyed teaching you, Edwin . . . goodbye.'

Edwin looked at Rownan with a frown. That sounded a bit final. 'I . . . I *am* going to be all right, aren't I?' he murmured, shaking hands.

'Of course – as long as you stay away from the crystal mines.' Rownan grasped Edwin's arm. 'Remember that and you will be safe.' When Edwin nodded, Rownan smiled. 'Good luck.'

Edwin and Perpetua watched Rownan walk away.

'How very odd,' Perpetua said. 'He could at least stay to see how you get on. You'd think he would after all the effort he's put in.'

But Edwin shaded his eyes to look elsewhere. Janus sat on a raised platform that stood beside the forest clearing. Next to him were Mersium and Ollwin. They were in deep discussion. Edwin turned to see Eifus and Dreifus hovering behind Perpetua.

'My lady,' Dreifus said. 'You must take your place in the seating area behind Janus.'

'Oh, yes – *behind* Janus,' Eifus added gravely. 'You must not sit *in front* of the king. Sitting in front of the monarch should not be considered under any circumstances. Sitting in front of His Majesty would cause a public scandal. Sitting in front of our ruler would never, never, never, *never* do.' His eyes widened, and he leant down into Perpetua's face. 'It is such nuggets of information that make our contribution to court so invaluable.'

Perpetua backed up slightly. 'I'm sure,' she said. 'What else d'you want me to do? The handkerchief thing?'

Dreifus nodded violently. 'Yes, of course. As you know, you will be required to perform second. My brother and I will stand to the left of the seating area – we will signal what you should do, and when.'

Perpetua crossed her arms. 'I *can* remember everything you taught me, you know!'

'We do not doubt that,' Eifus said pointedly. 'But a little aid to your memory will not hurt. We will of course be very discreet – no one will guess what we are doing.'

Eifus and Dreifus led Perpetua to the seating platform. A man in a very fancy blue uniform approached Edwin and bowed. 'Prince Auvlin,' he said. 'Please come and stand with the other competitors in front of our honoured guests.'

Edwin walked to the middle of the grass clearing and stood next to a young man who was wearing a long green cloak. There were probably a few hundred people facing them – most wore extravagant hats and they were all dressed very nicely, so Edwin decided they had to be the monarchs, lords and ladies of all the other territories. He stood up straight – he hoped he didn't look out of place.

'The orienteering discipline is about to begin,' announced the man who had called Edwin over. 'Ladies of the territories, please make your favour known.'

A woman in a flowing satin dress stood up and held up a white handkerchief. She moved her arm left, then right, then swept it down in a series of arcs. 'Lord Dulcia,' she shouted finally. 'I favour you.'

The young man in the green cloak walked forward and took the handkerchief. Edwin couldn't make out what he said. The woman and the young man bowed to each other, then he took his place back in the line.

Perpetua glanced at Eifus and Dreifus and got to her feet. Eifus started to move his arms as if he was performing secret dance moves. Perpetua took a silk handkerchief from a bag and held it up; she looked quite confident at first, but then looked back at Eifus and suddenly seemed rather confused.

Edwin saw Dreifus mouth, 'Like this!' and he flicked his hands from side-to-side.

Perpetua grimaced and waved her arms about.

'And this!' Eifus hissed in the loudest whisper Edwin had ever heard. Eifus stood on his tiptoes and made a series of flamboyant gestures. Perpetua shuddered and tried to do the same, but she looked like a chimpanzee trying to catch a fly. Edwin tried not to burst out laughing.

'And rest!' Dreifus shouted. His eyes widened and he clamped a hand to his lips.

'Thank God,' Perpetua mouthed, almost flopping down. 'I favour you, Prince Auvlin,' she wailed, jerking the handkerchief forward like a smouldering firework.

Edwin put on a determined face and strode forward. He took the handkerchief and bowed in time with Perpetua, but then murmured, 'What do I say?'

Perpetua kept her head down. 'What did you say?'

'No, *what* do I say!'

'Oh! Didn't Eifus and Dreifus tell you?'

'No!'

'My God! They are *so* useless!'

'Perpetua!' Edwin snarled. 'Just tell me!'

'You need to say "I accept your favour, madam".'

'Cheers . . .' Edwin murmured flatly. He stood up and announced, 'I accept your favour, madam.' He turned on his heel and walked back to the line, muttering, '*What* a shambles.'

There were eight more proclamations of favour, then each competitor was given a list of instructions, a map and a compass. 'You each have seven items to find in the competition area,' said an official. 'The winner of the discipline will be the first to return here with them all by the end of the day.'

'Sounds good,' Edwin said under his breath. He threw back his shoulders – he was really looking forward to this.

The official made some notes in a book, then threw up his left hand. 'You may begin!'

The group of young men surged forward, and at first Edwin strode to keep up – but then he stopped dead. No, he should check the first of his instructions before he went *anywhere*. He looked at the list, pinpointed his destination on his map and looked at his compass. 'This way,' he whispered to himself, setting off again. 'I can do another reading after a few hundred metres . . .'

As Edwin left the clearing he glanced back. Janus mouthed, 'Good luck.'

Edwin smiled. He was going to try hard for Auvlin, but he was going to win for the king!

Edwin was on a roll. He'd found the first two items – nothing fancy, just brightly painted stones with 'Prince Auvlin' written on them – very quickly. The third had been a bit more tricky, but the stone was now in his pocket and he was heading through the forest for the fourth. How were the others doing, he wondered? They'd have to be red-hot to be in front of him!

Dappled sunlight danced across Edwin's map as he opened it up. He traced his finger; the next item was ... *here*. Edwin folded his map, put it back in his bag and stepped onto a well-worn path. He walked for a few minutes before he took the water bottle from his belt, unscrewed the lid and took a swig. Boy, it was warm. It didn't help that he had to carry all this stuff around.

Edwin used his compass again, then changed direction slightly. He strode under a canopy of trees and peered in front. There was a soldier standing up ahead. He looked relaxed, but his hand was on his sword and he glanced around him every now and then. Edwin had seen loads of other soldiers today already – it was good to know they were there to protect him and everyone else taking part in the competition.

'Hello,' Edwin said as he approached the soldier.

'Your Highness,' the solider replied, bowing his head. He looked up with a smile. 'I am Hysterian too, Prince Auvlin. Are you progressing well?'

'Yes, very well,' Edwin said, trying to sound quite formal. 'What is your name?'

'Bradium, Your Highness.'

'Nice name!' Edwin replied. 'The weather's holding up, isn't it?' Bradium looked confused and Edwin added, 'It's not raining.'

'Yes. We are very fortunate.'

Edwin grinned. He'd like to have stayed for a chat, but he really had to get on. 'Thank you for . . . erm . . . looking after us,' he said. 'I'm afraid I must continue . . .'

'Of course,' Bradium replied. 'Good luck, sir!'

Edwin smiled and set off again. After a few minutes he dug around in his bag for something to eat, and pulled out a large piece of cream cake. Good job, he thought, taking a massive bite – today he was going to need all the energy he could get.

But Edwin suddenly ground to a halt and let the remainder of his cake drop to the ground. Someone was walking along the pathway ahead, moving very quickly. He could only see him from the back, but he looked just like him. *Or Auvlin.*

'Not *another* one,' Edwin whispered. He felt panic twinge in his stomach. What should he do? Should he follow this boy to see where he was going? What if there were other Umbrians around . . . what if the man and woman with the horses turned up?

Edwin caught his breath and scurried back along

the track to where Bradium still stood. The guard turned to Edwin, his eyes widened and he drew his sword from its sheath.

'What has happened?' he said.

'Go and get some help! Primus, King Janus . . .' Edwin blurted. 'There's someone – someone strange up ahead! I'm going to follow him – keep a track of him, but bring anyone you can to help me.' Edwin reached Bradium and grasped his arm. 'If I go off the path, I'll leave something on the grass to try and tell you where I've gone.' He spun around and headed back into the forest. 'Go – now!'

'Yes, Your Highness!' Bradium began to run in the opposite direction, his sword swinging through leaves and bracken.

Edwin's heart pumped as he retraced his steps. He tried to be as quiet as he could – he didn't want to let the boy know he was there. Edwin hoped he hadn't lost him . . . this could be *really* important.

'Yessss!' Edwin hissed to himself. The Auvlin lookalike was still on the path. He was walking as quickly as before, so Edwin had to up his pace again to keep in touch. Where was he going? Edwin swallowed against his dry tongue and glanced behind him; he hoped Bradium made it back in time to help.

As the boy walked further into the forest, Edwin took the map from his bag. He only had a vague idea of where he was, but he had a feeling there was a crystal mine around here. Edwin tried to find the last place he'd been sure of; but eventually he sighed, folded the map up and put it away. He couldn't risk trying to work out his position or he might fall too far behind.

Suddenly the boy turned and looked back. Luckily, Edwin was shielded by a bush that had grown over the path. The boy blinked and looked around him, as if trying to work out where he was, then he hoisted his bag further over his shoulder and stepped off the path toward some trees. Edwin hesitated. What was he getting himself into? But the boy was on his own, for now. And he wasn't carrying a sword.

Edwin crept forward, holding his breath, trying to keep the boy in sight. He fumbled into his bag, put one of the painted stones by the edge of the path then followed the boy into the trees, trying to avoid stepping on twigs and branches. After a minute or so he lodged the second stone in the V of a branch. He had only one stone left – how long should he wait before he put *that* somewhere?

But within less than a minute the boy suddenly came to a halt and sat down. Edwin edged forward and stood on tiptoe. The boy was sitting beside a large grassy bump, in the middle of which was a wooden door.

What was that? It looked more like an underground house, the kind you find in picture books; he expected to see a chimney trickling smoke into the breeze. Edwin lowered himself into the grass and waited.

The boy didn't move for what seemed like quite a while, and Edwin kept looking towards the path. Where was Bradium – surely he'd found help by now? And what was the Umbrian actually *doing*? The boy just sat there, eyes pinned to the ground as if he were deep in thought.

But eventually the boy got to his feet. He stood up straight, raised his head and seemed to take a deep breath.

'Mineralia,' he said suddenly, as clear as a bell. There was the sound of a heavy clunk behind the wooden door, and it slowly swung open. The boy hesitated, then stepped inside.

As soon as the boy had disappeared and the door closed shut, Edwin got to his feet. He stood still for a few seconds, listening. Hoping. There was no sign of anyone. There was nothing for it. He had no choice – he had to go in there on his own. Perhaps it wasn't a mine; the Hysterians would surely have more security than an old door and a password.

Wouldn't they?

Edwin ducked under a tree branch and approached the grassy bump. He took a gulp of water from his bottle and wiped his lips with the back of his hand. His mouth dried out instantly. He took one last backwards look towards the path, closed his eyes and said, 'Mineralia!'

Chapter Eighteen

The door swung open again. Edwin craned his neck and peered inside. This didn't look good. There was no cosy fireside scene, only a dimly lit passage that led downwards almost as soon as the threshold was crossed.

Edwin stepped inside, his shoes crunching on gravel. He looked around. Tiny flecks sparkled in the walls. Edwin swallowed. This was no woodland house, this was something altogether different. The door closed behind him and Edwin's stomach lurched. There was no turning back now. He just had to hope that the password – *mineralia* – would keep him safe from whatever was in here.

Edwin began to descend the steps. Almost immediately his legs started to tremble and he put his hands to the walls, his fingers running lightly over its sparkling surface. He stopped for a second, but couldn't hear anything, and set off again with his heart thumping. He started to shiver . . . it was getting cold; he must be quite a way down underground by now.

Eventually, Edwin stepped into a tunnel. It went straight ahead for a few metres, then divided into two. Both branches were dimly lit, and he could see no trace of the boy in either of them. Edwin swallowed. Which passage should he choose?

Right! Edwin decided suddenly. He was going to go –

But a strange sound made him change his mind. There was a faint hissing, like steam escaping from an engine. It died away and Edwin held his breath. Then it came back. Edwin turned on his heel. Yes . . . yes, it came from the left-hand branch.

Edwin forced himself to enter the passage, and he scurried forwards ten metres or so before coming to a stop. The tunnel widened and branched into several routes, fanning out in all directions. Out of the corner of his eye Edwin saw something disappear into one of them. He waited for a few seconds then followed. He didn't want to lose the boy.

The hissing grew louder then died away, as if whatever had made it had passed close by. Edwin edged forward and caught sight of the boy's back. He peered around a wall to get a closer look. The boy produced a small pickaxe from his bag then started to hack at the wall, his face contorting with effort as he slammed the point against the rock. Rubble sprung out and the boy scrabbled on the floor. He stood up holding a small crystal. He looked at it, put his in his bag then returned to his work, scouring the wall feverishly.

Edwin swallowed. So they'd been right – the Umbrians *were* after the crystals; that *was* what all this was about. But mining crystals one fake-Auvlin at a time? It didn't seem *that* much of a plan. Edwin glanced behind him. Perhaps Bradium had come back with help by now. The Umbrian was busy, he'd be here for a while. If Edwin could just get back to ground level and –

The hissing jumped to a blast and Edwin instinctively ducked. He looked up and around the wall. The boy had dropped his axe and was edging slowly backwards, his feet barely lifting from the tunnel floor. Something way down the passage was shining a beam of light. The beam was looping around and around and up and down as it if were coming from a searchlight, its glare reaching into every hole and nook of the tunnel walls.

The Umbrian crept back further still, his hands fumbling against the rock for guidance. Suddenly, the source of the light became clear to Edwin. It looked like a huge piece of jewellery, but it didn't seem to have any solid form. It reminded Edwin of a hologram – just like the invisible room at the castle. His eyes widened. The beam shone from the slightly blurred shape in the centre, semi-circles of metal protecting it on either side. Was the shape the image of a crystal? Edwin squinted, desperate to see. Then he realised *exactly* what the source of the light was. This was the ancient relic they'd seen in Rownan's book – the Armegia Charm! So *this* was what Janus had guarding the mines . . . not an old wooden door and some measly password.

Whatever duty the relic performed, it now seemed to paralyse the Umbrian boy with fear. He stood shaking, muttering under his breath as the hologram came closer. Its beam of light was now still, as if it had fixed on a target. It advanced very slowly, spotlighting the boy's shaky backward steps. Suddenly there was an ear-splitting shriek. The light inside the crystal intensified. There was a flash, the beam of light crackled white and the boy fell to the ground, clutching his face. The image of the relic retreated at once, its hiss shrinking away to almost nothing.

The boy rolled over onto his stomach and cried out in pain. Then he began to crawl, his face down to the ground. His fingers dug into the gravel, his nails scraping the hard, rough surface, and traces of blood began to smear around his hands.

Edwin felt as if a heavy weight was on his chest; he couldn't drag his legs to move. His throat began to press for air and he realised it'd been ages since he'd taken a breath. He opened his mouth and gulped, almost retching as he filled his lungs. The boy must have heard him, as he lifted his head. His left hand reached out, as if he were desperately looking for help. The boy's face turned slowly upwards, strangled grunts escaping his lips.

Edwin's mouth gaped and he stumbled back – the Umbrian's eyes were a mass of flaming red.

'Oh . . . god . . .' Edwin turned away. But then he made himself look round. How badly was the boy injured? What should Edwin do? No, there was no way *he* could save him on his own – this would need some magic. Edwin had to get some help. He turned on his heel and darted away, then slid to a halt; gravel flew in all directions and Edwin felt heat ebb through his legs. The relic was back – its hiss building; its bobbing, circling stream of light dancing along the walls and floor. It knew Edwin was there, and it was looking for him.

Panic surged through Edwin's limbs and he stumbled around a corner. He flung himself against the wall, his heart pounding. The relic's hiss grew louder still, the light from its beam bouncing to and fro like a laser show. Edwin managed to drag himself along a few metres, and dived into another turning. He looked at where he'd just come from – the light was growing stronger . . . he'd go the other way. He scurried along to the end of the passage and peered around the corner. There was only shadow. He could see the bottom of the steps. If he was quick he could reach them. Edwin looked behind him a second time – the light was growing stronger still. He lunged forward, but then cried out and clung to the wall. In the moment he had taken to re-check the other route, the relic had switched position.

This time, Edwin's legs felt as if they'd turned to lead. He tried to drag them backwards, but all his strength seemed to have drained away. He took short convulsive breaths and groped at his belt with trembling hands. It was pointless – he had nothing to protect himself with.

The relic's beam of light locked into position. It approached Edwin at a slow, menacing pace. It seemed totally focused. Edwin closed his eyes and sank to his knees. He was beaten. Was it really going to end like this?

The high-pitched screech rang out. Edwin's eyelids were wrenched open. He screamed in anticipation. His eyes were bathed in intense heat.

Then, nothing.

Edwin sat hunched, his eyes screwed up again, listening to the silence. Where was the pain? He slowly raised his hands. His fingertips shook as he held them ready. He was scared . . . what would they find? Edwin swallowed and gently dabbed his eyelids. He gasped and did it again, stroking lightly across the skin. They felt . . . *normal*.

Edwin opened his eyes, then shot to his feet. He could see. He could still see . . . *But how?*

There was a sudden sound of movement from way down the tunnel, and Edwin swung around. *The relic hadn't finished with him . . .* He swivelled madly, trying to work out whether there was anything he could use to defend himself. But it was Janus who emerged from the gloom, his eyes anxious, his face flushed. He rushed over to Edwin and pulled him into his arms.

'Are you hurt, my boy?'

'No, I'm all right,' Edwin murmured. 'But . . . but I *should* be hurt. The relic came and shone its light at my face . . .'

Janus caught his breath, put his hand under Edwin's chin and tilted it upwards. Edwin blinked into Janus's stare. The king looked as if he couldn't believe what he had heard.

'It was the relic?' Janus said slowly.

Edwin blinked. He wasn't supposed to know anything about this. 'It looked like something we'd seen in a book,' he said timidly. 'Your Majesty, I didn't mean to –'

'And it did not hurt you?' Janus said, almost to himself. 'I cannot understand . . .' He suddenly roused himself, let Edwin go and looked around. 'The soldier said you were following someone? Where are they?'

Edwin pointed back down the tunnel. 'Around there. The relic hurt him – it was *horrible*.'

Janus strode around the corner and Edwin followed. They reached the boy. He was unconscious, and Janus rolled him onto his back. His eyes were closed but it was still possible to see that he'd been hurt.

The king shook his head then looked up at Edwin. 'Another imposter! How many more – Will told us that *he* was the last one . . .' Janus picked the boy up in his arms, looked at his face closely then glanced around at the tunnels.

'Why has the relic not come to look at *me*?' he whispered. He frowned, then switched his stare to Edwin. He suddenly turned and walked away, the boy limp in his strong arms. 'Come with me, Edwin. It is not safe here.'

Edwin didn't need to be asked a second time. He gathered up his things and dashed to the steps after Janus. He looked back one last time before he started the climb. This was one place he didn't want to see again.

They reached the surface very quickly. Edwin emerged to find Ollwin and Mersium waiting anxiously and a dozen soldiers with their arms at the ready. Perpetua stood at the back, and she yelped as Edwin came into view.

'Oh, thank goodness!' she wailed, running forward. 'Are you all right. What happened? Did you –' But she stopped short when she saw Janus lay the Umbrian boy on the grass.

'Is this who you saw?' Mersium said to Edwin, kneeling down.

'Yeah. He was walking up ahead when I noticed him. I followed him into the mine.' Edwin scratched his head. 'I didn't know it was a mine at first, obviously, but he used a password to open the door, and I thought that I might be safe with just that. He was hacking crystals out with a pickaxe, and then –'

Janus raised a hand. 'No more – it is a secret of great importance. We will discuss it later.'

Edwin nodded quickly. He looked at the soldiers – *they* still thought he was Auvlin. 'Of course, Father.' He knelt down to have a closer look at the boy. 'His eyes . . . something happened to his eyes.'

Mersium reached over and put his thumbs on the boy's eyelids. The boy let out a whimper, but Mersium gently opened his eyes. Edwin braced himself for the horrific sight, but the blood-red mass had gone. The dappled light of the forest caught no colour, all there was to be seen was a glassy mist of opaque white.

'That's *horrible*,' Perpetua gasped. 'Is . . . is he going to die, like the other boy?'

'Yes, it seems so,' Ollwin said, putting a hand on her shoulder.

But Edwin had looked away. He was peering at the boy's arm, just where the sleeve of his tunic had bunched up. Edwin frowned and pushed the fabric further up. His eyes widened, and he said, 'Look . . .'

All eyes turned to where he was pointing. A faded purple bruise was on the boy's forearm. It took a while for Edwin to process what this meant. What this meant to him, to Janus . . . to Hysteria.

'This isn't an Umbrian imposter,' Edwin murmured. He shot to his feet, forgetting where he was and who might hear him. 'This is *Auvlin!*'

CHAPTER NINETEEN

Edwin looked at Janus, his heart sinking. He expected the king to start crying or shouting. But Janus just seemed to be confused. He got to his feet and stared down at the boy, his brow knitting together.

'No, Edwin,' he said slowly. 'This is not my son.'

There was an awkward silence, before Ollwin said gently, 'But, sire . . . but how can you be sure?'

Janus took a deep breath and looked over to where the soldiers stood. 'Leave us to talk,' he instructed. 'But stay close.'

The men filed away to where their horses stood, and Mersium, Ollwin, Edwin and Perpetua moved in closer to listen to Janus.

'What I am about to tell you is known only to me, Auvlin, Lorius, the Master Miner and those who work within our mines. It has been kept secret for centuries.' Janus thought for a moment. 'This must go no further. All of Hysteria's mines are guarded by something called the Armegia Charm.'

Edwin looked at Perpetua; her eyes widened and she went to say something, but he quickly shook his head.

'Anyone I permit to enter the mines must take part in a ceremony twice a year – during the ceremony the charm shines a light into their eyes, and it remembers the pattern and colour of its iris – which is as unique as the print on a man's fingertip. If anyone enters the mines and is not recognised, the charm intensifies its light and the trespasser is rendered blind. The brain is also affected . . . this leads eventually to death.' Janus looked down at the boy. 'Those from the Janus line need take part in the ceremony only once, but they are still permitted to enter the mines. There is, therefore, no doubt that this is *not* my son.'

A shiver ran down Edwin's spine. 'But this is the boy who's been living at the castle – all this time a fake Auvlin has been right there and we didn't know it!' He rubbed his forehead. 'So where's the *real* Auvlin, then?'

Janus closed his eyes. '*If* he is still alive, he must be held prisoner by the Umbrians. There can be no other explanation.'

Mersium grabbed the king's arm. 'He *is* still alive, sire. I can feel it!'

'I think Mersium is right,' Ollwin added quickly. 'The Umbrians have been replicating our prince – why would they dispose of an endless source of material for use in transformation? Prince Auvlin must be at the villa where the transformations take place. He must have been there when you rescued Will.'

Janus stared at Ollwin for moment. Edwin could see hope shining in his eyes. 'Yes,' Janus muttered. 'You are right, of course. That would make perfect sense.'

'So what do we do now?' Perpetua asked.

'We return to Emporium Castle,' Janus said gravely, 'and make plans to rescue my son.' He looked across at the soldiers. 'The competition must be stopped immediately,' he called. 'One of you must inform the officials. I need another man to help us with this boy.'

Ollwin went and spoke quietly to the soldiers. One immediately rode away and another came to stand over the Umbrian. Mersium organised the horses to take everyone back to the castle.

'What are you going to do with the boy?' Edwin asked Janus as they started off.

'I do not know, Edwin, but I could not leave him here. He is, after all, still only a young man. And even the worst of enemies – even an Umbrian – deserves a proper burial.'

The gates of Emporium Castle swung back. Edwin expected to see one or two people milling around, but instead there was a scene of great excitement. Lorius and six of Janus's elite guard were mounted on horses, ready to ride out. More soldiers stood staring up at the top of the castle, talking to each other in what sounded like tones of amazement. Bellwin stood behind them. He looked as if he were trying to listen to their conversation.

Edwin and Janus followed the line of the soldiers' gaze. Edwin glanced at Perpetua who pulled a shocked face. They were looking up at the secret chamber! It was there in partial sight, going in and out of focus.

Janus jumped down from his horse. 'Lorius, what has happened?'

'I was about to come to you,' Lorius lowered his voice and added, 'Let us go inside, sire . . .'

Janus pulled Lorius's arm. 'No! There was an incident at the mines . . . with the relic.' He looked back at Edwin and the others. 'More of us are privy to the secret now.'

Lorius looked over with disapproval. 'I see. But we should still go inside. Perhaps you would like the others to join us.'

Edwin shook his head as he followed the king. It was obvious Lorius thought that whatever had happened was all *his* fault. Typical – he got the blame for everything!

Lorius insisted on leading everyone to the top of the castle before he told them anything. They climbed the steps to the uppermost floor, and Perpetua scurried to catch up with Edwin.

'We're going to the secret chamber, aren't we?' she whispered. 'D'you think we're in trouble? D'you think Lorius knows we've been in there?'

'How do I know?' Edwin snapped back.

They emerged into the gallery, standing awkwardly, trying to look as if they had no idea where they might be going. Janus pushed past the others and walked forward. The door at the end was open, and it was possible to see up the flight of stairs to the ceiling of the secret chamber. The image of it was blurred and slightly shaky.

At the far end of the gallery two men were kneeling on the floor; their hands were tied and they were guarded by half a dozen soldiers. Rownan and Mornan. Edwin's eyes widened. Had they done something to the secret chamber? *Had* Rownan been trying to get to the charms all along?

'Er, scrub what I just said,' Edwin murmured to Perpetua. 'We're not the ones in trouble.'

Janus slowed for a moment with his fists clenched, then he strode to where Rownan and Mornan knelt.

'Rownan!' the king boomed. 'What have you done here?'

Rownan looked up. 'I have –'

'And what is its meaning?'

When Rownan didn't answer, Janus reached down, hauled Rownan to his feet and dragged him through the open door. 'Bring his son!' he yelled. Edwin had never seen him so angry.

One of the soldiers took Mornan's arm and followed the king towards the not-so-secret chamber. Lorius jerked his head, and Mersium, Ollwin, Edwin and Perpetua filed into the passageway.

'Don't worry,' Edwin said eagerly to Ollwin. 'It looks like you could fall through, but really –' he clamped his mouth, realising what he'd said.

Ollwin raised an eyebrow. 'Yes, Edwin?'

'Nothing!' Edwin squeaked. But he could've kicked himself. And Perpetua looked as if she could have done much worse.

The chamber was just as it had been before. Nothing seemed to have happened in there. But Edwin had only taken a few steps into the second room, Saleena's room, before his legs wouldn't take him any further. He felt Janus's hand on his arm, guiding him away from the doorway so that the others could pass through.

'Oh . . . oh, my . . .' Perpetua whispered. Edwin sensed her stumble back, but he couldn't take his eyes off what was in front of him.

A woman sat where they'd left Saleena only a week

before, wearing the same simple white toga and delicate gold brooch. But instead of a fresh, bright-eyed beauty, she was a hunched, decrepit being – paper-thin skin folded and wrinkled over a bony face and body and white wispy hair hung in thin strands from a crusted yellow scalp.

Edwin swallowed. She looked like a walking corpse – older than he'd ever imagined anyone could. If this was Saleena, she must have aged by every one of the two thousand years that she'd been in the secret chamber.

Saleena slowly raised her head, and peered at Janus through glazed, hooded eyes.

'Your Majesty,' she wheezed, her words barely audible. 'I am sorry . . .'

Janus knelt down and took her hand.

'The relic,' she whispered. 'They disarmed it . . . for a few minutes.' She closed her eyes and seemed to drift off. Janus took Saleena's weight and laid her on the stone floor, cradling her head on his arm.

'Do not try to talk,' he said gently. 'You –'

'No, sire,' she said breathlessly, 'I must tell you . . . it is my duty.' She took a gasp of air. 'They disarmed the Armegia Charm, but I saved it . . . it is working again . . .'

Edwin raised his eyebrows. That's why he'd remained unharmed. Rownan must have disabled the relic just as it was approaching him in the mine. He bit his lip. Wow! *How lucky was that?*

Janus smiled at Saleena. 'Then you have done well, my lady.'

Saleena could barely shake her head. 'No, I have failed. I had to save the charm because I did not protect it. They knew the password, I did not expect . . .' She raised a shaky hand and brushed her fingers over her mouth. 'My beauty has vanished . . . I am dying.'

Edwin looked at Perpetua. She looked close to tears.

'You die with honour, Saleena,' Janus said gently.

Saleena closed her eyes. 'If I am truthful, sire, it will be a blessing. Many years alone with only my reflection for company . . . youth became so little comfort.'

Everyone stood still as the rhythm of Saleena's breathing slowed. She took her last breath and then let out a long, soft sigh. And when Janus lay her head on the floor, there, in her ancient face, was a little of the beauty she had clung to for so long.

CHAPTER TWENTY

Silence filled the room. Edwin felt it might have gone on forever had Primus not suddenly rushed in. He looked at Saleena, but quickly recovered himself and grabbed Janus's arm.

'Sire, there are more sightings in the forest. We should go. Now!'

Janus glanced at Mersium and Lorius. Both nodded, and within seconds everyone was rushing back along the gallery.

'Take the woodsman and his son to the cells,' Janus called back. 'Place six guards upon them. Every other available soldier should follow me . . .'

At the stables the horses were saddled, and very

soon everybody was mounted and ready to go. Edwin and Perpetua told Bellwin as much as they could about what had happened before they filed into the courtyard. Two divisions of Janus's elite guard joined the party and the rattle of their arms filled the air as horses stamped on the stone cobbles. Edwin felt a strange mix of excitement, fear and pride.

The main gates opened and Primus led the procession out into the open. Hundreds of people who had come to see the triathlon had now gathered around the castle.

'Quickly!' Primus yelled, pulling his jittery horse to a stop while the guard galloped past. 'Our destination is the eastern edge of the forest, where the Leigh River alters course.'

Edwin turned to Perpetua and Bellwin. 'There's a *mine* there,' he said, wide-eyed.

Primus's horse charged off to take the lead again. Janus followed and suddenly everyone was cantering away from the castle. Edwin's chest was so tight he could hardly breathe, and Perpetua's face was set in a worried scowl. It took an age to get to the forest. Edwin wondered if whoever had been sighted would still be there. And what if they weren't up to anything after all – was this just a big waste of time?

Primus and Janus pulled their reins as they approached the forest, and Edwin tried to catch his breath as his horse slowed to a gentle trot. Primus pointed right and steered into the trees, with everyone following. Once the last of the elite guard had filed into a clearing, Primus jumped down.

'The sighting was just beyond the river,' he said. 'I will take three men with me.'

Once Primus and his men had disappeared, Janus turned to Edwin. 'I did not think to ask you, my boy – are you willing to join us?'

'Yeah – of course,' Edwin said quickly. He glanced at Perpetua. 'And if *she* didn't want to come we'd have heard all about it by now.'

Janus smiled at them both.

Very soon one of Primus's men came running back through the trees. 'Bring the men, sire, as quietly as you can,' he said breathlessly.

Janus pointed into the forest and the horses started a steady walk into the trees. Within a few minutes Primus and the other soldiers appeared.

'I have seen a man and a woman waiting on horseback outside a mine,' Primus said, keeping his voice low. 'And there was a third person – a young man wearing a metal helmet.'

'The man and the woman are the ones we saw in the forest!' Perpetua hissed. 'This young man must be yet *another* transformed boy . . .'

Janus shook his head. 'A replacement for the one Edwin followed to the mine.'

'Yes,' Perpetua agreed. 'Dealing with two fake

Auvlins in the same day – who'd have anticipated *that* when we got up this morning.'

'We should take our places,' Primus cut in. 'We must be ready for whatever happens.'

They kicked their horses forward, and made their way to a thick line of bushes. The elite guard stopped a few metres behind, but everyone else settled under cover of foliage. Edwin peered through gaps in the leaves – sure enough, the same man and woman he'd seen before were waiting outside what looked like an opening to a mine. Janus turned to them all with a finger pressed against his lips. Edwin and Perpetua exchanged glances, then looked at Bellwin. His mouth was clamped, as if he hardly dare take a breath.

Minute after minute ticked by. Suddenly, Perpetua looked rather panicked – she started to move her hands quickly, as if trying to use sign language, flashing her fingers in tens until Primus raised a hand.

'Look!' he whispered.

A young man – who, of course, looked just like Edwin and Auvlin – had emerged from the entrance. Edwin held his breath, waiting for him to drop to his knees or bring his hands to his face. But . . . *but he looked all right.* In fact, he walked forward perfectly normally and held up a small grey sack to the waiting woman.

Janus frowned. 'Saleena must have been wrong,' he murmured. 'The Umbrian is unharmed – the Armegia Charm must still be broken.'

But then something else caught Edwin's eye from across the way – a flash of metal. He made out a face amongst the trees. Another . . . then another. Edwin's gaze streaked from left to right and back again.

'Blimey,' he croaked. 'They've only brought an army . . .' He looked at Perpetua – that was what she'd been trying to tell him.

Janus had spotted them, too. He sat up and kicked his horse.

'Yes, Edwin, but so have we!'

Janus's stallion thundered through the bushes and everyone followed his battle cry. The elite guard poured through the undergrowth with their swords raised.

'Edwin!' Bellwin yelled above the din. 'Come with us!'

Edwin turned to see Bellwin and Perpetua veer right and trot up an embankment – it looked safe there. Edwin shook his head. He might not be a real prince, but that wasn't going to stop him. He turned to fight with the rest.

Umbrians streamed into the clearing. They all looked much the same – tall, broad, muscular, with the same savage expression, and the same wild staring eyes. But the oddest thing about them was that they didn't make a sound. With eerily calculated precision, each focused on one Hysterian, then charged forward like an automaton. Edwin's hands began to shake. They wanted one thing, and one thing only. To kill.

Suddenly a ring of elite guardsmen swarmed around Edwin, shielding him from the battle. His horse was jostled from side to side. Swords clack-clack-clacked in the air, sunlight flickered on metal like camera flashes. The Umbrians were silent but the King's Guard cried out loud and clear. It was a huge effort just to keep the enemy at bay.

A blade swept down and a Hysterian fell from his horse. The Umbrian wielding the sword now focused on Edwin, but another guard quickly filled the gap. Another fell, then another; but every time a new man replaced him. Edwin glanced over at Janus. The king had ordered them to protect him.

Bellwin and Perpetua were still safe, perched on top of the embankment. What about Mersium? Edwin craned his neck. There he was. He had the fake Auvlin by the collar. Primus was steering his horse left then right, hacking through a line of the enemy.

A horse reared up and Edwin almost fell from his saddle. He lurched left and caught a glimpse of an Umbrian only a metre away, wide-eyed, snarling silenty, slicing the air with his sword. A Hysterian blade cut down into the Umbrian's arm, but the injured soldier didn't flinch or utter a sound. He swished his sword again, blood spraying with every turn of his wrist.

Edwin heaved himself up despite the fear surging through his legs. There were countless cries of injured

Hysterians. More guardsmen were going down. Were the Umbrians too strong for them?

Janus's horse suddenly appeared. The king struck out. An Umbrian fell twisting to one side, directly facing another. Suddenly, the other Umbrian stopped, as if stupefied. He didn't move. it was as if he'd been turned to stone.

Edwin held his breath. He remembered what they'd seen in the villa.

Then, in the thick of the battle, it started to make sense. Everything around Edwin seemed to slow as his brain put the pieces together. An answer gradually formed . . .

'They can't look at each other!' Edwin suddenly bawled. 'Make them look at each other . . . force them to look!'

But nobody could hear him. Edwin looked around, dismayed. How could he make them understand? Without thinking, he jumped from his horse. He scoured the ground before him . . . where was an Umbrian body? Over there – just a few metres away. Edwin launched himself through a gap and landed by the corpse. There was the thump, thump of hooves on grass as he tried to lift it. Something swished to his left and Edwin ducked. He crawled behind the Umbrian's head and put his hands underneath the shoulders. The eyes stared blankly up at him, a horrible smell rose from the mouth. Edwin swallowed, sick to his stomach, and hoisted the upper body onto his chest. The head fell to one side. Edwin took a breath and looked up. He'd been spotted. The Umbrian focused on Edwin, his eyes filled with fury, his mouth drawn over blackened teeth.

Edwin shuffled forward, still propping up the body. The Umbrian lunged towards him, raising his sword. Edwin reached for the corpse's head. The Umbrian was ready to strike. Edwin lifted the head as the blade began to fall . . .

The Umbrian froze. The sword fell from his hand. He stood, seemingly paralysed with confusion, then crumpled and hit the floor.

Two or three Hysterians had seen what had happened and leapt from their horses. They dropped their swords then lifted bodies from the ground and held them up. One by one Umbrians fell. More corpses were found and whole lines began to fall one after the other. Hysterians twisted round and round, lifting the chins of the dead to meet the gaze of their fellow Umbrian soldiers. They fell in perfect order, like hay in a crop circle.

Soon there were no Hysterians fighting. Every one of Janus's elite guard had grabbed hold of an Umbrian body. The king stood in amazement, watching the rest of the enemy presence fall without another drop of blood being shed.

'In the name of Hysteria,' Janus said as he watched

the last Umbrian hit the ground. 'I have never seen anything like this.'

Primus and what was left of his men looked around, their swords held at the ready. Edwin assumed they were looking for Umbrian survivors, but not once did they need to use their weapons. Bellwin and Perpetua, realising the fight was over, rode down from the embankment, they dismounted and Perpetua grabbed Edwin's arm.

'Are you OK?' she said anxiously. 'I couldn't bear to look, until Bellwin told me I had to and that I wouldn't believe my eyes. What happened . . . it was incredible!'

Primus picked his way over the bodies. 'Edwin showed us what we had to do,' he said firmly. 'Once again, it is *he* we have to thank.'

'How did you know, Edwin?' Bellwin asked.

Edwin shrugged. 'The Umbrian soldiers reminded me of the boys in the villa – they all looked pretty much the same, *and* they didn't make a sound. Then Janus got one of the soldiers, and when he fell he looked into the face of another one, and it seemed to . . . to sort of paralyse him. I remembered what happened in the villa – when the boys looked at each other – and I made the connection.'

Bellwin shook his head. 'Perhaps the boys at the villa are the Umbrian army in waiting,' he said gravely.

'How awful,' Perpetua said. 'The rumours that the

Umbrians have been farming humans – it seems it's true.'

Primus slid his sword into its sheath. 'We have lost many soldiers, sire, but there are no Umbrians left alive . . .' He looked over to the mine. 'Apart from *him*.'

Edwin caught his breath. He'd almost forgotten about the boy! He followed Janus and Primus to where Mersium was standing. But as Edwin came closer, he could see that Mersium wasn't guarding the Umbrian. They were standing side by side. Mersium looked hesitant, as if he didn't quite know what to say to the king.

'What is your name?' Janus said. There was uncertainty in his voice.

The boy looked at the king. If Edwin didn't know better, it was a look of admiration . . . almost love.

'I am Auvlin.'

'What?' Janus whispered. 'But the charm . . .'

'Father,' the boy said, his voice shaking. 'The Armegia Charm is *working*.'

Edwin froze, his throat clamping shut. The boy had said *Armegia Charm*. There was only one way he could know about that, and only one way he could've got out of that mine uninjured.

The boy *was* Prince Auvlin.

CHAPTER TWENTY-ONE

They were back in the throne room. Edwin was still reeling slightly as he sat next to Bellwin and Perpetua – so much had happened it'd been hard to keep up. Janus was on his throne with Auvlin and Mersium by his side. Ollwin, Lorius and Primus joined them, then the king sent for Rownan and Mornan.

'I have a feeling this story is a complicated one,' he said sadly. 'And their part in it will not be a small one.'

'Too right!' Edwin said. 'That's spot on!'

'Your Majesty,' Perpetua added. 'He said you were exactly right . . . and exactly right again.' She blinked. 'He said it twice.'

Edwin kept glancing over at Auvlin, who returned

his look with a smile. Well, he thought, this version was a lot more friendly than the last. Hopefully he'd have the chance to get to know the real Auvlin before he and Perpetua went back home.

Everyone sat up as Rownan and Mornan were brought into the room. Rownan's eyes met the king's without hesitation. But, as always, Mornan's face was turned to the floor.

'We are here,' Janus said, 'to hear the full story of what has happened to us all.' He reached over and squeezed Auvlin's hand. 'You may begin.'

Auvlin looked around the throne room and smiled. 'I can scarcely believe I am back,' he said. 'The last time I saw my home and my father was the day I left for Meticulla with Bellwin – to see Wizard Brolin.'

Bellwin frowned. 'Are you saying that you were taken by the Umbrians on the way to see Brolin? We were so heavily guarded . . .'

'No,' Auvlin replied. 'I was taken *after* I had seen him. Do you remember – we had stopped to eat, and I suddenly decided to look at one of my father's mines. It was only a few minutes from our path, and I rode away before any of our guards could come with me.'

Janus shook his head. 'You are too headstrong,' he said sternly.

'Yes, Father . . . I know,' Auvlin replied quietly. He looked back at Bellwin. 'It seemed that Umbrians had been following us for the entire journey – they saw me alone, followed me to the mine and replaced me with one of their own. Our guards caught up eventually, but by that time I had been taken.'

'Blimey,' Edwin said. 'So had the Umbrians been waiting for you to leave the castle – looking for *any* opportunity?'

Ollwin coughed. 'Did the Umbrians take you so that they could transform more and more boys into your image?'

'Yes, Master Ollwin. At first they used a supply of hair that was taken from my body when I was in the mausoleum so many months ago – but the Umbrians needed to make *many* copies of me and they did not have enough.'

'And the object of all that,' Perpetua said, her eyes glittering. 'Was to get at Hysteria's crystals – they knew you were allowed to go into the mines.'

'Of course,' Auvlin agreed. 'But even the copies the Umbrians made from me could not enter without being attacked by the Armegia Charm. It infuriated them.'

Perpetua shot to her feet. 'You know why that is – however many copies are made of someone with transformation, they will always keep the *same one* physical feature of the original. With you, it must've been the iris of the eye.'

'Which was *just* the thing needed to get into the mines,' Edwin said slowly. 'Now that's what you call a dose of bad luck!'

'That makes sense,' Ollwin said. 'The notes of Agnetha's visit to the villa said that after a boy had been transformed, his eyes were always examined very closely.'

Edwin nodded. 'But the only way they could know for sure was by the fake Auvlins going into a mine.' He huffed. 'Unfortunately for *them* . . .'

'So what about the Umbrian that took Auvlin's place here?' Perpetua asked.

'I would guess,' Auvlin replied, 'that he was transformed with one of the last strands of hair from the mausoleum. He was needed to replace me, so he was not sent to the mines.' He rose from his seat slightly. 'It suddenly occurs to me, Father – what has happened to him?'

Janus gestured for Auvlin to sit back down. 'He *did* visit the mines this morning.' He thought for a moment. 'He knew we were aware of what the Umbrians were doing, and that we were planning to take action. The Umbrians had no way of communicating with him – I had him under guard – so he did not know what he should do. Perhaps he worried that the Umbrians were going to run dry of crystals, so he shook his guards and took it upon himself to plunder the mines.'

'But he had no idea what would happen to him when he tried . . .' Edwin murmured. He looked at Auvlin. 'The relic got him and he died.'

They sat in silence, before Perpetua said, 'You know,

I thought there was something funny about him when we first got here!' She crossed her arms. 'He didn't recognise me, remember – that makes sense, because if he was transformed with hair taken from the mausoleum before the *real* Auvlin woke up, he wouldn't have had any memory of me.'

Edwin pulled a face. 'But he knew who *I* was . . .'

'He was always going to recognise you – he knew you looked just like him!'

'Yes, of course!' Bellwin burst out. 'In the days after our consultation with Brolin, Auvlin kept asking me about everything that had happened since he had been "killed". He kept going over and over it . . . I thought his memory had been affected by Brolin's second course of treatment. But now I see – he was trying to find out everything he needed to know to be a convincing Auvlin. And, of course, he would *still* have had a lesser sense of direction, because the Auvlin that had been treated by Brolin had been taken to Umbria.'

'*And*, Edwin said, 'once the fake Auvlin realised *that* might get him found out, he persuaded you to bring me here. He told *us* that Brolin's treatment hadn't worked straight away – which Brolin backed up accidentally – but he didn't say that to Janus because he didn't want the king to start checking things out.' He looked at Perpetua. 'The fake Auvlin didn't ask Bellwin anything about *you*, because he wasn't expecting you to come with me.'

Mersium sat forward. 'We must be thankful the plan was discovered – had Janus and Primus not seen you three riding in the forest that night, the triathlon would have gone ahead with Edwin taking Auvlin's place. Janus would not have known, and the Umbrians would have carried on replicating our prince, hoping to one day produce the Auvlin they needed.'

Edwin scraped a hand through his hair. 'I'm really sorry,' he said to Janus. 'I wasn't sure about coming back in the first place . . .'

Janus rose from his throne and walked over to Edwin. He put a hand on his shoulder. 'Your intentions were good,' he said. 'And who knows, if you had not come, events could have been much, much worse.' He smiled. 'Besides, it has been *so good* to see you again.'

Edwin grinned. That was all he needed – the king's approval. It made him feel ten feet tall.

Janus ruffled Edwin's hair, then turned on his heel. 'Rownan,' he said suddenly. 'Why did you enter the secret chamber?'

Rownan looked the king directly in the eyes. 'It was an act of revenge, sire.'

Janus stopped dead and frowned. 'Revenge?' he repeated. 'An act of revenge against *me*?'

'No, Your Majesty,' Rownan said quickly. 'You have been the kindest and most generous of monarchs.'

'Then why would you want to destroy the Armegia Charm?'

Rownan took a deep breath. 'Because it destroyed my family, sire.'

Janus glanced around the room, as if he were looking for answers. All he saw were blank faces. Edwin looked at Perpetua, but she just shrugged.

'Explain yourself, Rownan,' Janus said.

Rownan glanced left at his son, his head bowed as usual. 'Mornan worked in the mines for three years. He was a good miner – he toiled hard and was never absent. He enjoyed his work. He was proud to be of service to Hysteria. But then . . .' Rownan swallowed. 'But then, one day – seven years ago – the service to which he had decided to devote his life did not take proper care of him.'

When Rownan paused, Janus said softly, 'Tell me, Rownan – tell me what happened to your son.'

Edwin could see tears in Rownan's eyes. The woodsman gathered himself and continued. 'He went to the secret ceremony, so that the Armegia Charm could renew its recognition of him. But Master Miner Grettel did not perform the ceremony properly.' Rownan reached over and put his fingers under Mornan's chin. 'Look up, my boy,' he whispered, pushing gently. 'It is time to tell our king . . . there is no need to be afraid.'

The room grew quiet. Edwin held his breath. Mornan lifted his face and slowly opened his eyes. They stared up, dead and blank, the same misty white that had covered the eyes of the Umbrian boy.

'Mornan went to the mines the next day,' Rownan said, barely above a whisper. 'But he was unprotected and the relic blinded him.'

Janus said nothing for a while, his face was set with disbelief. He looked at Lorius. 'Why was I not told about this?'

Lorius got to his feet. 'I did not know, sire.' He glanced around the room. 'Did *any* of us know?'

'No one else knew,' Rownan said. 'Grettel was at the mine when the accident happened – he was able to use a magic remedy quickly, and without it Mornan would have died.' He shook his head. 'He was as sorry as any man could be, and as he had saved Mornan's life, I promised that I would tell no one of his mistake.'

Perpetua shifted in her chair. 'I . . . I found a book in the library,' she said. 'It had a sentence scribbled in the margin about an accident during a secret ceremony involving "MMG". Master Miner Grettel . . . that must be him.'

Edwin sat up. 'You visited his wife, Rownan. Did Agnetha have a part to play in this . . . did she help you?'

Rownan nodded. 'Grettel was so racked with guilt by what he had done, his health declined, and within a year he fell very ill. On his deathbed, he made Agnetha promise that she would help me find justice for Mornan. Once Grettel had gone, I wanted to take revenge on the Armegia Charm itself. Agnetha already had a special interest in all sorts of magic, but Grettel told her everything about the charm – how it worked . . . how to find it . . . how to break it. Agnetha felt obliged to help us, and she passed the knowledge on to me.'

Janus got up and started to pace the floor. 'So, you returned from your visit to Agnetha intent on destroying the Armegia Charm. You knew that many troops would be away from the castle the day the triathlon started, and you planned your attack.'

Rownan didn't flinch. 'Yes, sire.' He looked up. 'I know I will be punished but I beg you to spare Mornan. He has endured enough misery.'

Janus stopped still and stared at Rownan.

'And you have not suffered?' He strode forward and grasped Rownan's shoulders. 'I cannot blame you for what you did,' Janus said, his chin trembling. 'He is your son . . . he is *your son*.'

Edwin swallowed. He looked at Perpetua. She blinked furiously.

Janus reached down, took a dagger from his belt and cut the ties that bound Rownan and Mornan's wrists. 'There will be no punishment here today,' he said. 'You are both as free as ever. And I command that we try to find a way to restore your sight, Mornan. That is the very least I can do.'

Rownan gazed at the king; he seemed to be lost for words. But Mornan reached out, as if he were looking for Janus.

'Thank you, Your Majesty,' he said softly when they finally brushed hands. 'Thank you.'

'Do not thank me,' Janus replied. 'It is the actions of two young people who have brought everything to light. Once again, we have Edwin – and Perpetua – to thank for saving our crystals and, ultimately, our kingdom.'

Edwin stood up, his cheeks staining red. 'Oh, no . . . no,' he said, raising his hands. 'This isn't like last time. I didn't do much of *anything*.'

'Edwin!' Perpetua whined. 'Credit where credit's due . . . just accept a bit of praise for once. It doesn't come your way that often.'

'Thanks!' Edwin huffed, folding his arms. 'Just tell everyone, why dontcha?'

Janus laughed. 'And, of course, we owe you another debt, Edwin. Tell me, what did you use the last wish for?'

'He didn't use it for anything *important*,' Perpetua said quickly. 'He used it to help his friend.'

'I . . . I don't want anything,' Edwin said slowly. He shrugged. 'I just wanted to help you, Your Majesty. I'm happy with that.'

Janus didn't say anything. He just looked at Edwin and smiled. That was payment enough.

CHAPTER TWENTY-TWO

After considerable nagging from Perpetua, Edwin decided that they'd stay in Hysteria for a few days before returning home. Edwin spent a lot of time with Auvlin – something which Janus seemed very pleased to see – and Perpetua spent most of *her* time in the library or badgering Lorius to show her some experiments.

'He told me to get lost this morning,' she moaned at one point. 'Just shows that *anyone* can pick up a bit of slang at Templeton Grove Comp!'

Janus decided to hold a special lunch in Edwin and Perpetua's honour before they went back, and that they should choose the menu. Whatever they did in the kitchen, it worked a treat. The lunch was, as Edwin put it, wicked. And there wasn't too much fuss – no big speeches, no claps on the back. Just lots of smiles and lots of warmth. Best of all, Edwin got to sit next to Janus, with Auvlin on the other side of the king. To Edwin, it almost felt like a meal with his family. His *proper* family.

When the hour came, Edwin didn't feel as ready to return as he'd done the last time. What had changed, he wondered? But then he thought about Nat, and football, proper books and DVDs and ketchup. He decided there was a lot to look forward to at home, too.

Once again Edwin's maturing charm was reversed, and he and Perpetua showed up in the throne room dressed in their school uniform. Auvlin grinned when he saw Edwin.

'Apart from the strange clothes, you look just like I did two years ago!' he cried. 'How odd,' he added, 'that we are so much alike.'

Edwin and Perpetua said goodbye to everyone but Janus, and Eifus and Dreifus came scuttling into the room just in time to shake hands.

'Perpetua,' Eifus gushed. 'We had no chance to congratulate you on your winning performance with the kerchief. Such elegance! Such style!'

Edwin pulled a face. 'Er . . . you *were* watching the same girl?'

Perpetua ignored him. 'Thank you, Eifus,' she said pointedly. 'I'm sure it was all down to you two!'

Dreifus peered at Janus. 'All down to us?' he said, raising his voice. 'How very kind of you – it is so nice to have one's abilities as a teacher recognised . . .'

Janus crossed his arms and sighed. 'Eifus . . . Dreifus. You need worry no longer – you may return to your duties as tutors to the court.'

The brothers looked at each other and giggled, and as quickly as they had scuttled in, they scuttled away again.

Edwin watched them disappear into the passage, and raised his eyebrows. 'I know I didn't want a big fuss, but *last time* they could hardly bear to see me go . . .'

Janus stood beside Edwin and put his arm around him. 'I wonder if they feel as I do?' he said gently.

'And how's that?' Edwin asked, leaning against the king.

'That we will see you again, my friend.'

A shiver ran up Edwin's legs, and he smiled. 'I . . . I hope so.'

'Me too!' Perpetua jumped up, flung her arms around Janus's neck and kissed his cheek. He wiped his face, then began to laugh.

'Sorry about that, Your Majesty,' Edwin said. 'She's a bit over-excited.'

'Edwin!' Perpetua said, completely oblivious. 'I've been meaning to ask you – when we enter the vortex *we* choose what time we go back to, don't we?' She tilted her head. 'Can I decide this time? Is that OK? Pleeeeease.'

'You've got a nerve!' Edwin said. But then he shrugged. 'Yeah, all right. Just don't do anything stupid.'

'Great! Thanks. Come on then, let's go!'

Edwin waved to everyone, then he gave Janus one last hug. 'Goodbye . . .' he said managing to fight the temptation to cry.

'Goodbye, Edwin,' Janus replied. 'Until the next time.'

Edwin stepped back and half-smiled. 'Yeah,' he murmured. 'Until the next time.'

Then Perpetua tugged his hand. The next thing Edwin knew, they were standing in front of the vortex.

'So, Einstein,' Edwin said as he prepared to step in, 'what did you decide?'

Epilogue

Templeton Grove Comprehensive School
INTERNAL MEMORANDUM

FROM: Mr F. Harper, Year 4 Science Teacher
TO: Mr I. M. Smellings, Headteacher

15.9.2011

I have just marked the Year 4 test papers from last week. Incredibly, two students achieved 100 %.

One pupil was Perpetua Allbright (no surprises there), but the other was the last person I'd expect to even scrape a pass – Edwin Spencer.

Apart from the fact that he HAD to be cheating,

something is worrying me. You'll remember that Mr Lorius (God forgive him, wherever he is), awarded Spencer an A in last year's winter term report. Consequently, Spencer's mother came to see me every day for six months, enquiring about his progress and asking for extra work. She believes her son is a scientific genius, and nothing I said would convince her otherwise.

I ask you – no, beg you – for permission to lower Spencer's test mark. A drop of around 85 % should do the trick. If this matter is not addressed I fear two things are inevitable: 1) Mrs Spencer will once again be beating down my laboratory door, and 2) I will have to double my medication.

Yours,
Frank

About the Author

J. D. Irwin (who also answers to Julie) started writing *Edwin Spencer Mission Improbable*, the first book to feature Edwin and Perpetua in 2001 when pregnant with her daughter. She'd been writing grown-up fiction on and off for many years, but maternity leave gave her a chance to have a serious stab at something else. She soon discovered that writing stories for children was much more fun, and from then on didn't want to write anything else!

www.jdirwin.com

Also published by Catnip . . .

J. D. IRWIN

'Calling Master Edwin Spencer! You are summoned
by the court of King Janus of Hysteria. Pass through
that vortex that appears before you!'

Edwin Spencer has enough problems at school as
it is, without strange voices calling him into another
dimension! But when he is sucked into the peculiar
kingdom of Hysteria on a secret mission he feels
very at home. This could be his chance at last to be
a hero, even if he does have Perpetua Allbright,
school swot, as his sidekick.

You can find out more about J. D. Irwin
and other Catnip books by visiting
www.catnippublishing.co.uk